SLEEPING WITH
THE ARTIST

Published 2007 by Page-Addie Press - Great Britain
Copyright © Susan Blanshard 2007
Cover artwork © Bruce Blanshard
Cover and layout: Ngo The Quan
First Edition

ISBN 978-0-9556509-1-8
A CIP catalogue record for this book is available from the British Library.
Sleeping with the artist/Susan Blanshard

This book is a work of fiction. All characters and all actions and events, motivations, thoughts and conversations portrayed in this work are entirely the product of the author's imagination, and any resemblance to actual persons or events is entirely coincidental.

2

SLEEPING WITH
THE ARTIST

SUSAN BLANSHARD

Susan Blanshard was born in England. Selected poetry from *Fragments of The Human Heart* and *Evidence of Obsession* appears in World Literary Review: Projected Letters, and her essays, *The Content of Water,* published by ICORN International Cities of Refuge. *Postcard From Hanoi,* published by International PEN Women Writers'. *Postcard from China Beach* appears in the Fourth Anthology, *Our Voice, Nuestra Voz, Notre Voix,* International PEN Women Writers', 2007. Her book *Sheetstone: Memoir for a Lover,* Spuyten Duyvil, New York, was published in 2006. Susan lives in Hanoi with an artist.

For John High: a rare literary friend and witness

You tell yourself that it is a woman you hold in your arms, but watching the sleeper you see all her growth in time...

Laurence Durrell

Clea

I am accustoming myself to the idea of regarding every sexual act as a process in which four persons are involved. We shall have a lot to discuss about that.

S. Freud: Letters

A book must be an axe for the frozen sea inside us. That is my belief.

Kafka : Letter to Pollak, 1904

PREFACE

Among the one hundred and twenty graduates at the Paris Academy in 1974 was the Artist, Mané Dumas.

His most recent exhibition at the Hanoi University of Fine Arts, brought together works covering a period from 2000-2007.

The paintings that make up this extensive retrospective exhibition remind us, the critics wrote, or suggest something of his experiments with the exteriority and interior of an infinite landscape of female form, such as the deeply personal *Black Modona (1998)* to the bold linear *She (2004)*. An art of mind and body, his works reflect the complexity of his love of the organic woman and, his flowing brushstrokes, powerful calligraphic lines and heavily impastoed surfaces of his paper: Rhythms of his heart, alive, the lines pulsating with a clear love of a woman that might have been lost forever in the cacophony of experiment of change, or in the transience of love before it becomes permanent art.

The large works that make up this exhibition have energy and vitality, they wrote, that is, if one did not know the artist, you might suspect these paintings were the product of a much younger man.

ALSO BY SUSAN BLANSHARD

Essays

Postcard From Hanoi (2006)
The Content of Water (2006)
The Sleepers (2006)
Verde (2007)

Poetry

Sheetstone: Memoir For a Lover (2006)
Fragments of The Human Heart (2007)
Evidence of Obsession (2006)
Perfume River (2007)

Anthologies

Postcard From China Beach (2007)

SLEEPING WITH
THE ARTIST

SUSAN BLANSHARD

Two or three months since arriving back in Hanoi, the heat of September still continuing, sweat on his body, not wanting to move from under the ceiling fan. Late afternoon and this damp humidity was not the only thing that woke him. The songbirds in bamboo cage. Someone playing a melodious tune on a fipple flute. Her breathing. It sounds like the river, he thought, like the blood reaching inside her body. A breath of wind. Then no sound but that quiet inlet of water.

Looking at her laying beside him, he could draw her as he saw her now, observing the symmetry of her bare limbs, the tanned skin burnished and in parts, where skin forms into dimples at the lightest pressure or that the touch could first hold, and as he touched that exactness of shape, in the fall of it towards the thighs, where the waist ends and the rounding swell of the hips begins, then slide over a smooth surface and her thighs felt polished, copper in original colors, when he slid his hands between; and when he reached out and touched the beautiful growth of dark hair, in short soft curls, but it was no ordinary feeling, wheat fell into his palm and ripened and he separated the glistening seeds out with his finger. He looked around; there was no river, no field, no wind, only a woman sleeping.

On the table beside her, hundreds of pages bound in leather, the rich red of women & secrets she had written while she was away. Scarcely daring to breathe for fear of disturbing her, he softly disengaged himself from her arms, leaned over without waking her, so quietly that he might have passed for a dream, and he took the folio.

10

Pillows behind his head, he lay back down, holding in his hands that part of her composition which his fingers now opened, there, imprinted, as if it was a private survey or a secret manual and he is turning the filmy pages, then who can express the fire in his eyes when she speaks of him.

She had said nothing to him about the content of her book. All the pages from the book of the fifth folio number two hundred and thirty. Three are blank. Three engravings of text, one page folding out, numbered woodcuts, music and specimens of alphabets in the text. Folded, cut or torn; paper has memory and her words, intercepted in that moment, were his. The chronicler of her own secrets. Her words turning slowly on their own journey, some traveling backwards, some leading forwards to other things. Afterwards, the closed shutters, warm bodies, volume of roses.

He looked at her face, the eclipse of her dreaming eyes, it seems the name of the woman has been eliminated from the text but secretly, he thought, all women are disclosed in these margins. The power of a beautiful woman, with which it is said, like the moon, she borrows her second light from the man. This soft candescence allowed him to read her words.

Pale yellow light slipped into the room through blue leafed ghost palms and between wooden slats in the closed shutters. How night turned into another and as she writes down what she knows, she leaves a series of illuminations in the air - angelic shadows at the end of her fingertips, I must include the silver moon isolated by time, oxidized light sparked against the reef of stars, encircled the rooms and keeps me awake...

I

I had already dreamed of having a place in a man's life, and when I found you, I was just seventeen. I woke up in your bed, an afternoon at the end of solitude, a night and morning shared, (this as my small book will be interwoven) rose flower tea & wheat toast for breakfast.

I wanted to love you into words before the shadows of the future slipped past us, to love you when we knew each other, simply as lovers & dreamers, for loving you is what I discover, masculine smell on a throat (musk & leather) and one summer remember us as color, (honey & bronze).

The air in a room diffused with freesias: the flowers, (double red blooms, amorously intermingled), arranged by instinct, perfumed for pleasure. There is a flower preserved for a long time in the room of memory, here the flowers never lost perfume, the light through the window never faded, a glass vase on the sill, always full. With a faraway sound of one dog barking & rain falling outside the room. And a sound of murmuring, inviting that soft sadness which is the beginning of pleasure. Any moment triggers an image, and emotion repeats itself.

For it is said, this bond and place, carries the weight of desire, one man and woman stealing all the desire of the world, if you wrapped a blindfold over my eyes, tapped the velvet bones with your hammer, there are enough moments inside me, to take over my body, for me to detect your fingers (trailing dreams) over my skin. So much of you is part of me. Lover. You know this.

These pages are the footprints on the grass. I am absorbing all the moisture with my bare feet. I am taking responsibility for the dew there. City winter. I am sleeping on a mattress in a disused brothel, evenings in the streetlight room. Rethinking all the secrets that pull you into me, I am pulling the sheet over your shoulders; I am turning the page on my feelings about the man, and me, and that receptive repeated intimacy. White sheets strewn with roses. A garden of scent at the edge of earthiness.

Some of the fragments you knew: Cold. Color. I am carving your name in the wind. In the winter room of a Victorian house, and from when the house was built, sugar sacking nailed to rough kauri planks, wind whistled through gaps... sounds like voices. The bed... it will make a noise... they will hear us!

First night, the sketches were rapid (you copied no one) and the way you moved my limbs and then you finished with pleasure. We see into the room, the sepia & melon-skin walls are visible when the windows are open: but if you look through the windows in order to see us kissing, you see moving shapes instead, as two animal mates, we hibernate under pure linen. The king bed mattress striped in white and black cotton, shaping itself to curves we pressed into it. So I will sleep with you there for six to seven months, beginning in the winter when the light falls behind the mountain at four-thirty in the afternoon and the nights last fourteen hours.

And so, he thought, that afternoon, the first kiss I gave you was enough to reach you, irresistible enough to take your heart and disturb its delicate secrets, as its rhythm echoed mine, deep ties of desire, so tight & delicate they may break without us noticing.

The Artist realizes that she has written every intimate detail of what happened in each bedroom. What goes on behind the door. His blue shirt on the floor. Undressing down, until he was standing naked. In this private life, it became instinctive. His torso & all binary biochemistry of the body. Commingled. Her mouth & this French kiss, as they intersect and interlace in the passage.

He came as close as he could and discovers something else. She would go further, she knew, she knew that two embodied essences may feel more than thin love, from sex to soul, from soul to thought and from the soul to sex again. Perusing her anatomy of desire, seeing his own passion written here, he asks: who told the scribbler to reveal private affairs. Is this her natural weapon? Soft words. Their power can pull down the bloody moon; turn back the sun, make rivers flow upstream. Doors are no match for the binding; toughest locks can be opened by her look.

Dark oak bed ends carved in flowers& acorns and in the distance, the sound of Mozart violin refrain, playing loudly, a pulse, as if the composer understood each physical movement. It is necessary to note, between those movements, as his body pressed against her.... it was like making love to a part of her poetry.

There is something simple about the Artist's images; they are almost like poems about private places he would like kept secret, but has decided to give a hint about what these private places might be. What is impressive about this triptych of a bedroom scene is the individuality of each vertical piece, which, on its own can be a painting by itself. When put together, they become a powerful piece that transports the viewer right into this room.

III

Let me retrace the curve of your eyes while you dream, what becomes of us while we are sleeping. I believe in the wedding of it… we made first love and later I would be dreaming of you. He started reading about the first afternoon, where their relationship began, half a page and the room changed. The unmade beds were images of intimacy he returned to (if he described heaven… he would be her astronomer). When he came into the room, his senses were pulled towards her. Inflaming him, as if she had studied the most seducing ways, without appearing to have studied them at all, waiting for first pleasures without seeking them.

He walked over to the bed and sat close to me, staring me in the face, whose eyes seem to say, I will teach you the meaning of love& sex & trouble, this secret vow, repeated thousands of times, more than first moment I enter you, center you: open to me, intimate space and the voice whispers, here it is, we are in this together.

(list)
Charcoal
Paper
Canvas
Brushes
Palette

Oil
Stone
Fire

His First Woman is part of this same series. This work comprises a series of charcoal drawings, Studies for First Woman, depict a series of rounded shapes with soft edges.

The sun casts light onto the corner in a lattice shape, as if a sunbeam is shining through a slated shutter. Dumas's image is filled with falling light. Should we be concerned at shadows... as if a stray piece of sun was falling into the room?

The ceiling and walls of the room were covered with wallpaper, of ghost palms and leaves: in the midst was a bed with white linen & pillows, a hothouse of white petals, ribbons and lace, as if it grew against wall.

Let him undress me and paint what he pleases, and I'll not interrupt him except to imprint more kisses. For Mané, you caught my eyes, like fire on a hill... maybe seen, as I saw myself, the heat there I found, one look from you and all my body burning. A few leaves jangling in their intactness with tiny rust holes. Burning wild grasses & wildflower brushed on the walls and you in this room. I have a match. No lighter.

How long have you been waiting for a man?

I did not answer him, my experience of a man existed in abstract, a look, a note, but he smiled and kissed me, he made my face hot and I knew where this was going. He noticed my cheeks.

You are blushing.

The surface texture and muted colors and tones of his charcoal work suggest the natural woman without her masks. Noting the sensitivity in her. With his lyrical line and color, Mané creates a beautiful geometry, of dream & surrender. Her hair tousled and long. He noticed the sensitivity of her hands as she pushed her hair away from her eyes. A sense of movement, the tension of colliding forces with the woman. From her, he draws inspiration. Bringing to mind the myth of Pygmalion and Galatea, the Artist's desire arouses the model into breathing life and an unexpected reciprocity on the lips when he kisses her.

IV

I wanted you. So I did the only thing I thought I could do with my mouth. I kissed you. I kissed lips that formed those beautiful words, every inch of your mouth with my tongue, to find a secret cove where your voice lay hidden. The unnumbered kisses lost in a crowd of warm kisses on lips as warm, and eyelids of eyes that swim in liquid fire, he passes his hands over skin like genesis of rays over the whole earth, and his lips for some time remain, as if impossible to move away. And this time his tongue in my mouth, I loved his way of kissing. Imprint of your lips. A man who kisses like fire summons my soul back. I took his tongue under mine, an untranslatable feeling in a mouth. Then he stroked my neck, tiny beating drum of pulse. On a throat.

And I love to smell your musk, as it drifts over my body and it fills my mind like incense. I feel as if some fragrance spilt over me, like musk held in dust and air. Like the room where we first made love in, it keeps returning, the long afternoons with the moments of bright or fading light casting shadows on walls and ceiling, dividing my thoughts between what was and now is. These thoughts slip out easily, like my arms from this shirt when I undress in front of you.

I saw, your jawbone fixed like the slant of the air when you saw me watching you, as your smile broke into an arc of love with your lips. The smile was unfamiliar to me. Then you smiled again but it is the weight of your hand pressed in the small of my back that arouses me. As close as getting to this, knowing the secret feel of you, I need no longer dream it.

It feels like a red-hot fire shut up inside a bone. Nothing can contain it and only a flow can cool it. If I understood then, his desire to enter, there, between virgin and finished woman. Why he kissed me again (which explains why there are so many studies of the same figure) waking from a dream. Into the arms of a man who woke her sleeping body. One million years and every instinct broke into life, the blood of women; blood that boiled in her veins began to swell parts of her virginal body. He painted her giving herself to him. Then long shivers of passion shook her. The artist had never known a woman like this.

The Artist opened his eyes and blinks as if he saw me, not just through a cage of dark eyelashes but further on, though moebius veils of time. He wanted the lover, in her nakedness. He gave her more. He gave in.

He could look across and see her hips slightly raised as if someone had placed a small pillow in the small of her back. Sometimes the Artist would feel himself touching her with his hands, and he would hesitate before he moved away, as though he had been making love to her- it was not a matter of letting something come about passively but of him bearing down on her image.

The model is lying there, her body unfolded to her full length, the Artist moves his hand down her legs, as though to brush off a fall of sand, before, behind, up between, up inside and her thighs & her body moves under his touch. At such movements, they were already lovers and the waves eddied around her, wetting stray strands of hair and wrapping them like strands of seaweed around his neck. A kiss in the water, and the scarcely perceptible salt in a mouth.

Your kiss on my lips carried by physical incantation, every kiss held, every release, unreal. Blindfolded destinies. This complete seduction. I only know this secret of sacrament between. And tomorrow, who knows when the fire returns emptied ashes, reminiscent winds that will blow the air and our voices back together. Like incantations and waves. In this breathing in, among the breathing out. I will find you; the wind blowing through our infinite existence, pushes our souls together. Side by side. You hold me, then stand away. I want to feel your body warmth from a distance. By this warmth and only this, we have existence, the Artist said, *by love, which belongs to us.* Whole segments connecting one of us to the other. Where I want to be found by you, as the one traveled. All the doorways leading to cities of memory or through windows shuttered in the cool breezes in our empty rooms. Can I step over... move the sliding door?

As I quietly found the key once and unlock the door once, move deeper into the room, I know the room, all of our chambers, thinking of the dwelling, light in each archway.

I lay beside you, a woman speaking to your very existence, each breath folding in and out of your lungs, a heart beating, repeating perfectly, caged by bones, whole life repetitions in circadian & primordial rhythm. Traversed by your body span, part muscle, part sinew. Strong steel of a man in the night. Like iron ore vice: hold me tight. Into the pulse, the moving and breathing, subtle like a shape of forged or softly welded parts. I want to be filled with you, sinew, muscle, bone; nothing breaks the feeling of you. *(With sketch)*

Note the movements and how she holds a pose, with her arms and her legs outstretched, then begins to laugh. Her shoulder blades, in a movement, change the rocks of her spine. The land belongs to her past. In the first sketch, so many thoughts abandoned, there was a pile of stones on the floor.

Watching the artist from his bed, she sees him, as the scene itself, the Artist standing there, holding with one hand the side of the canvas and with the other, a sable brush...and the model kept protruding her lips, as a woman who wants a kiss from him.

The Artist detects how a smile collects itself at the corners of lips and spreads across boundaries of a mouth, a migration like oil spread on top of water. And slowly paints a brush line of crimson, the paint pulls softly through sable, spreading out and leaving a moist stain, as though her lips were watercolors on a paper kite, he will feel her tug away from him, rise up and float out of his grasp- that one day she may set her smile loose on other men.

He will watch her until he looses sight of her. And if he waits for her, she will be back, a smile flashing at him across the room. The Artist will loose this woman and find this woman again.

The light changes. The light casts a grid shape onto the wall of the studio, like a sundial, it casts a slow shadow across the room, but unlike a sundial, it gives no time of day. Looking at her, he was not sure whether it was his own shadow, or whether they were casting shadows over each other. It is like working in earth or clay, he thought, you can take away or add to it and when the shadows are cast, in this dirty bronze light these last shadows stay in enduring form, forever remains of day. These nocturnal imaginings pressed against your skin. In which the skin registers shadow as a degree of black, as if you read my mind, remembering the shift of the shadow, as if you let a stranger in.

She compels the Artist to paint a complete scene with her, the orange-yellow perfectly balanced perspective, more weight at the bottom... golden triangle coming together with azure stretch of sky. This atmosphere is blue, was it light stolen from above? Not that it mattered one way or another. He begins with a single color, adds several more colors, so the motion of mixing pigment changes, from primary to original shades. When he paints her, there is light in her hair and her skin is tanned; she enters the painting from left to right, a differentiation between the light along the top and soft brown between. Then the paint stops.

Does she move when his mind composes a still picture of her, as in landscape and in the portrait of her face? The Artist thinks so and he seems right. It may be that his still compositions borrow their mobility from spheres of creation because material composition needs motion (kissing her, his hands to her waist).

When he finishes he inhabits the picture with her, the canvas, reinvents the artists room into a field. She is earth, the voices, the silk & velvet and painted flowers; she is Latin words and clouds -- all those beautiful things floated on waves of music as though in another world. Vinteuil's sonata…aerial and fragrant…Swann's Way. Cesar Franck's Sonata for piano and violin. Verdi, I will remember you when I hear these, Mané said.

Can I make love to you again?

I was thinking how to tell him that I could not stay. That it was late in the morning and too early in my life for anything repeated and permanent. I should go, I thought, but did not find myself speaking those words. There was a power in his asking. A politeness and he didn't wait for an answer. And the feeling so exquisite and tender, beyond all refusal.

I heard myself speaking…what I love, I am.

I find these fragments with you since you invited me in. Not invited, so to speak. In opening door and entering, in this brief passage where dreams cross over dream-crossed space, before falling in love with you. There was witness in the month: of ice paper celandine— first flower seen in March after winter thaw. Others loved you and have fallen through, discarded when you left, his face pressed against a window. Writing a poem in breath fog, rusted with nostalgia.
They loved you too much or not enough, he said.

How do you love another?

There are rules, he said, looking me in my eyes. To love you must first open your heart. You need to feel more for another person than

21

your self. The essential thing is to enter love deeply, held by immaculate tourniquet, bound by it as it tightens and transforms you. Stay in love, long enough until it is familiar as a room.

V

Sometimes in the beginning, in that bare room, his room, climbing up the wooden stairs, there could never have been a simpler place for lovers to be than this, he locked the door from the inside, in the intense honesty, we talked. This was not our sole preoccupation. The virginal student of love in a man's bed, touching his body, then her fingers on his thigh are a trigger, as if she has touched him before. I forgot. I only intended to stay with you a one night before returning to my own room, but then the way you kissed me and the moment my head touched the pillow. All the clothes that lie on the floor and spread over everything a white sheet she had thrown off (a body in perspective).

She enters his senses through the pupil of his eye. The sister of nature passes through this tiny entrance, (the measurement of a figure) through a pinprick the vast image of all he sees in her, he senses her cells and moisture, between his eye and her, atmosphere she suffuses in him. He thinks in perspective. (The Artist studies angels) though when he looks into her eyes he does not see one. But, he sees the image of a man smiling back. In this way, he occupies a small part of her, but you cannot see the edges of his lips or any familiar detail of his body. So you do not recognize the man she sees, unless his features are defined, he can be any man, seen through her eyes.

Later, he surrounds her with light and shade, (four drawings done with a pen) but a woman carries her own light and shade. Sometimes he paints her in bad weather, or in deep dusk as evening falls, the walls tinged with black and the shadow of the roof eaves falling

22

through the window, across the studio floor. Beyond the wall, the width of summer days folding into ghost palms, and in that light, the falling of one day into the next, in that slow burnished light, her face looks perfect. (A woman with beautiful hair) And the man in her eyes is smiling.

In this drawing, the light is left as distant as possible, a soft light came through the un-curtained window, then vanishes before the Artist composes her, *legs slightly apart,* and the sheet gave an upward twist, and the sheet was iridescent silk, and the sun pouring through it painted skin of her thighs with flickering patches of light. Beneath it, there was magma warmth; he could follow the gradual shadow cast between her thighs by the fold of the sheet until it was lost in a darker shadow and as she moved her legs, her hips buried themselves in the folds and then, gently rose out of them. Where he smells night and morning mingled with her honey, of wild grasses and him. Mané's painting suggests landscapes. There is in his surfaces, something of the color of savannah, landscape that is marked by the elements- wind, rain, storm, that dislocate both the natural world and human presence.

In the warmth of the room summer makes, all the sheets crumpled by the unquietness of lovemaking, tossed off in sultry heat until both bodies lay naked. The palpitations and vibrations as though life was playing inside her. She seemed to know exactly what she wanted. She was lying in the full light of the sun and by the glare; he could see the visible weave of the sheet, the pores of her skin, even her eyelids when she shut her eyes. It maybe that he transfers the sheet and her body in chromium white, as tissue-like images, the rising of her hips, like a bridge arching between the two pieces of cloth, the movement, or the residue of movement of his hand as he touched her over these, the imagined scrims of sound.

For a while, (describe each bed) two single mattresses pushed (together as intimate nature) on a natural pine frame, slatted and uncomfortable, like sleeping on the bones of a skeleton, (some objects possess bony relief), walking into the upstairs room, the haunted air, it is dark, possibly supernatural (are you scared?) the temperature cooler in the thatched cottage; (cold projects itself) further than the room, (medieval) into the place of crows & poison berries ripening in hedgerows.

In that wild lovemaking, with no practical purpose, his drawings watched us. But our exposé made their eyes close. Lust formed of our own bodies, caught between the nakedness, at the first boundaries of sex and the last fence-line of sleep, the scent of apple blossom outside the window, the muscle of the moon swelled into evening, the threshing in white sheets, one dog barking in the distance.

Things that happened in my life were brought together through you. Everything around here. The warmth on the face as if you and I were closer to life's blood on those nights. In that room, I dream, I gave you a child you did not ask for. The night we could conceive, (boundaries we no longer define) a kiss, given and taken, perfectly received, and love strengthened by all that is given, the moment was all; a fertile night when our shadows moved, the strength of the moment, for a thousands of tiny cells rendered in the heat; children who were born, like fruit borne by the straw. I found they were there in your arms, with your name, babies blanketed for winter, like tiny hibernators belonging to us and the room, (introduce a great fire) the fire is red dyed deeply into the blood & color black oakburn of night. It is the only color. Between you and me and the fire, in the half-light, the edges of flames light up our skin. In the morning, the smell of this freshly showered man and warm toast.

VI

He draws her naked. For the soul, the Artist said, is changed either by the passions of the body or according to its own passions. Drawing requires practice, it requires a repertoire of positions that the Artist asks her, in sketches where she stretches across the bed, then leans back so he can draw her face.

Where do you first begin when you draw a woman?

Color the lips, measure the pigments, the moment before the color of beginnings and after all: ending are all clearly illusion. Arbitrary, the Artist added. You reach another life then find yourself leaving again. Her first kiss betrayed the natural woman, her body born into passion. The Artist came close to telling her a greater truth; that sex incites him to draw her, in order to render her naked, and, in doing so make love to her.

I would begin with your eyes, he said, as a light to the rest of your body. Like stars to be looked at, but never reached.

The Artist is looking at the way an image can be moved within the room, the model's hips, the folded sheets, the falling light, and the Artist also looks at the interior image (a small pull laterally causes an image to smile).She was standing close, he behind & she raised her head & he bent down & kissed her long & slowly on her throat...then tilting her head towards him, her lips parted, a kiss on a mouth, litmus of kiss, of red cherry, this time, ...the tongue pushed into the moist center parting on a mouth... he seemed to be exploring her. *The rest was symmetry...* Like the first time you spoke my name. (No). You did not speak. It felt like your voice broke my name, breaking it open, like an ancient seal.

Why does it seem so easy?

I read your lips. Your mouth is made of the same flesh as your heart is; your words are the same as your thoughts are drawing you as an outline, first. And by drawing you, I can hardly draw my own breath. To have pictures of you changed into life, see the fire and warm you, then kiss the flame as it catches alight, then burns me. But if I am to draw you, you must keep still.

It is easy for me to stay still, but impossible for you to draw still.

If he was drawing a woman lying on the sheet, one side of her body exposed to the light, is interwoven with sunlight, until heat appears to penetrate the right side of her torso. Closest to the window, her breasts, her hair falling over her right shoulder appears flooded in blue. If this is true, she may be the river. The wind. If she becomes changed into the colors of things close to her. He will feel rain in his eyes. Wind pulling him back. But this does not happen in this room.

VII

During the past ten years, the Artist drew a series of drawings, mostly of women who posed in his studio, his strength (and it is said that he is very strong), his strength shows itself in the intensity of line and in their scale. The drawings are extremely large. The canvas of *Woman in the artist's studio is 2 meters x 800 .Woman and the flowers is 1800 x1206.* Yet it is a small inventory of pure beauty. And in that one, the arrangement of the interior, fabric and flower, is a filmy piece of lace whose pattern is a flower, it is not her body, but liquid surface beneath, in which still sex-warm, the lace slip clings to her thighs. For this he used black ink to adorn the arms, feet and shoulders of the model with patterns preserving the glyphs of sexuality influenced by iconographic forms, notably the altarpiece and the

26

Pieta, and early cabalistic writings, the script lifting veils and prayers when masculine and feminine elements were in harmony.

Does an artist draw from lonely or lust?

Both. Life is never without a scar.

So you would draw my features true to life.

The tiny scar under my lip?

A scar is a point of reference for the eye, whether received as a tattoo- or naturally found, like fortune lines on an open palm; scars reveal a woman's past and identity -perhaps even read as her future. It's casualty of scars discovered, as if by accident. Attention to detail, strands of hair, silver scar do not escape the Artist's eye. Mané reads her scars as crucial pieces of information.

It has always been this way between us, the Artist said. In the semi dark rooms we read each other naked. Scars, each scratch: sensing tiny perfections of your skin where you hurt yourself once. A haze of blood, a piece of pain. Each pigment, each tattoo, each bruise a moving scar, an accumulation, as if you never heal. I want to discover the origins of you. Touch the scars.

When I see something beautiful- a throat, a belly – the hand wants to draw it. The desire to make an image – I seize the woman as the object of imagination.

I think I would paint flowers as perfume dabbed behind your ears, the sweet smells of fresh violet colors, when women want to attract a man, women do not wear their own scent but the scent of flowers, I have smelt a garden on your throat, the Artist said, drawing in diversity of color is sweeter, wild garden knots tied up in colors, unlike you, flowers can neither speak nor think of scars.

I am reminded of the moment he entered his art, its altitude as he soared above two flowering islands it revealed a pattern of colloidal scars to suggest healing after injury; the graphic quality is a strong element in the work.

I have drawn you in my heart: drawing. (No) contrary to my art, imprinted, and with such pressure, that nothing can erase the deep embossing unless I rub my heart out.

When her limbs, her breasts were drawn with delicate ink, her hair falling leaves; he placed his hand and felt her heart beating under the bark; and the branches: he held them, as if they still were limbs. In the orchard of another garden, where, as this is the pre-image and after-image; outlasting all images, a while later, the glide of the transparent over the solid image: a sheet that held her, falls over the woman - cut; the shadow of the sun moving behind the shutters -cut; four o'clock and the rain falls on the roof of the room -cut; both words and memory have visual content, moving between life and death and in the waking dreams and worlds we touch. Is it the brushing of one image against another?

Private images blurred to "painterly" effect in his usual manner, on a large scale, give viewers nowhere to hide. Sittings go on for hours, days, sometimes weeks, as the model holds a position until, growing tired, her hands and limbs falling into a narrative expression of the painting process. In his paintings of a singular female nude, her body, muscular and contemporary, unveined with classical real-ism. *Dumas appears uninfluenced by anachronistic works of great masters he studied, like Apelles and Caravaggio. His canvas is emptied of all but the most necessary objects. Dumas's nudes remind us of our own mortality - or at the very least, the divide of the wound separating flesh and blood from canvas or paper.*

In a recent review of the Artist, it was said that Dumas's recent paintings are dramatically flawed.

All the portraits in the recent series are the same, with both arms open and with the open mouth facing either left of right. I saw all the brushstrokes. They are about a woman. If she met in his studio, if she put orchids on the bed. The flesh and perfume. I have seen a woman whose very wound hides pain, when blood gushed out, I have spent years listening to this zoology; but I had seen the woman in the room under the roofs as it encloses intimacy, where everything exists, gestation that is secretly human treasure, rubies and gold hidden deep in the garden, it begins as fertile ribbons tied to a man.

When looking at the work in reproduction, one becomes aware of the rigid structure underlying surface. Certain muscles give greater emphasis to the geometry of the composition or a pattern of light and dark. This structure is evident when looking at her naked body.

Her body is silhouetted against the night. The dark gives the work tension. From closer in, a shiver in her body is answered by him, as he presses his hips against her. He lets go his breath in a sudden rush. As if he has been holding his breath for a thousand years. The River. She saw his floating heart. The witness. She has seen him bleed.

The under painting, over which red has run thin drips of paint. During this process, the canvas is turned on its side and paint is pushed into ridges at the edge of the tape. There is also an intermingling of line and pattern, which alludes to something deeper- to the interconnectedness of all things. This woman. The one he configures love for. The mathematician. She knew the things that counted for happiness. The woman. She took the seed of all and the glistening core of him. The Shrine. Of all her bones and what is in her soul. The woman. The real one. Closer to her, he surfaces.

White canvas is silence. I heard the paint dry. Still life. Still. I have heard the echo of white, the white shadow of lead behind the paint, when inspiration comes to meet you; it comes from soft land beyond the bone. A look from her eye settles like a thought in his heart. One of her wooden doves. One of her ivory swans. He sees them in the long shadow beyond the bone.

I understand white, the Artist said. I've seen dreams crumble, snap and break like well-preserved wishbones. Been blinded by rice grains drying in oriental sun, dazzling blindness of white powder snow. The whites of nautilus shells, eggshells, and crushed pearls. There is bone white, burned gritty and gray. The white of ghost. I prefer to make my own white from the stones. He pointed to tiny white stones in cardboard carton. Stones as large as a fist, others the size of a baby's fingernail.

Where did they come from?

The sea. They were calcified and carried by oceans.

I watch him rub paint stones, the fragments rich and oily until the surface is completely smooth. That is where you get to? Your canvas, still unpainted. As if only someone who was an artist could find pure colors. Last night, I dreamed I was surrounded by powdered pigments of every hue, I picked them up before they slip out of my hand. The five pigments for her skin, the crimson for her lips, the powder in a bowl already brightly stained, blue azurite for her eyes, and black made from charcoal to draw the outlines of her curves. All flowing out. Draw her. Paint her. Open the paint box and paint until you run out of paint. What then? life. But then there will always be merchants selling sachets of malachite and orpiment and all the precious pigments you need.

With an extended palette, Mané comes up with endless possibilities. He places his model in melodramatic rooms for a series of hotel bedroom paintings using acrid colors, oranges, pinks, reds and yellows, where the sheets unsparingly voluptuous on the bed and abandoned garments on the floor provide a carnivalesque framework for the private dialogue between the Dumas and his model.

A robe appears in the foreground, an Oriental snapshot of embroidered birds and peach trees. And the model slipped her arms through a sheath of silk sleeve. She felt like perfume had

30

spilled over her... what created the small stain that looked like ink, a tiny stain that mysteriously disappeared and reappeared in different places.

In my heart's mind, there is no abacus to count these moments. It isn't just days of light but these images of interwoven things, an image of your hair on the pillow falling over your eyes as you turn your head, turn of your face, opening your mouth, as if the body gives up the secret of its stones.

As the Artist was refining his thoughts towards her, as pencil sketches or studio studies for oil serve a purpose for a composition, so his thoughts break into facets, like torn cut and colored papers as integral components, the collage of thought defined by overlapping his thoughts with hers.

Can I ask you a question?

If you answer me with another.

Who do you love most in the world? Mané asked.

No man has asked me that.
The thing that is most like you.

My drawings?

Yes. The sketches in the red journal.

I have shown no one but you, the Artist said.

VIII

Expressions of desire have appeared in Dumas's works, using rhythmic lines to show women who posed in natural, intimate and uninhibited poses. His paintings, erotic and sensual, a reverence for the female form, as if the artist is elevating the object of his desire to a spiritual plane. As often, his passion is direct, with a candor that has shocked his critics as his works face inner memory, deep in symbolism and metaphor.

Here, the whole room has been transformed by memory. As if repainted, refurnished and reconstructed from original desire, the Artist remembers the melon walls ripe and warm with the stems of candles burning. The white sheet dyed lime green and hung like a single curtain of thought. Bits of old furniture came back, the whore's red mattress supported on four perfect columns of demolition yard timber. When inks are applied to paper, paper reacts, attracting and absorbing moisture & tones to create images that are partly controlled by the artist's intention and partly due to the paper's own sensitivity.

I see women along the living earth whose power the air, earth and sea resembles. I have seen her color, as late afternoon, the sun catches fire as sunsets turns the world to gold, before she falls asleep in amber light, echoed in mirrors, I have seen her as perfume, exotic aromas and eastern sandalwood on the wall, she whispered : here women could set wet silk on fire, and then she did something else. Speaking to the plants, stars and earth, the caché of words determining fate, curing sickness, and aloneness, stirring vital passion, the arousal and seduction of all men.

Some of what they tell us is heard in the body. For you and what we do in the night together, loosen the knot and see what happens.

His woman, pure line and light precisely rendered a testament to designations of the masculine and feminine elements. As a series of mutual images of lovemaking, neither lost or hidden in their sexuality, intentionally using a brush weighted with ink. Here's the earth of a woman he temporarily inhabited. In the index an accelerated learning system and instructions for the Divine. A synthesis of the science of love. Each was a message for him, like a string of summers.

For this city, she wrote, lies within a river bend. Its name means a bend in the river. But in some confusion, the city has had at least seven names and sometimes the boundaries were moved. A hundred yards from Saint Joseph's cathedral, down a narrow alley, there is an ancient pagoda. When they rebuilt it in the 15th century, in the foundations of stone, they found a statue of a woman who was then worshipped in the pagoda. Two hundred years later, the walls needed rebuilding. Each time they were rebuilt, the walls collapsed. So the men dug the foundations deeper and each time they did, another statue of a woman was found. When enough women were unearthed, the walls held fast.

This was a place of rules: climb down from your horse. Walk on foot. Carry the corpse of the past over your shoulder. Two thousand years of time, because it knows the way. The path leads to a second courtyard. A gate left open should be closed. This was a place of offerings. Of cakes, rice, tea. Black ink. Of women merging with rock. For it is said: diamonds look better on her finger than in the quarry. North of the old city is White Silk Lake, which once had a palace with a hundred roofs. It is reached by a narrow lane lined with stalls, women selling breadfruit & roses & paper votives; giant snails and fried & fermented shrimp cakes. The museum is down this street, thousands of rusted arrowheads and three bronze ploughshares. The obscener parts of war, she will not claim these barracks of bloody histories. Land of filth or flowers, know the world the women believe. Assassins fans silk and sandalwood, unhinged they flutter and locked they kill; so it is written on deadly silk, this metamorphic poem, chrysalis verse begins to show a beautiful structure of death wings. Some were poisoned by rivers of rain. Call them tears. All caused by sad are salted and bitter. Sometimes I heard her crying but those were sweet tears given by love and birth. This distinction of honey. In knowing this, he saw her for the first time. He begins to know her, as if he never knew her, though he has slept with her since she was seventeen. As she moves towards him, she moves like a sleeper who turns in her sleep and pulls him closer. She makes him forget there was a night in which he was ever asleep.

PART II

I

There is Venus the Artist made at the Academy, small enough to fit in the palm of a hand, a curvaceous limestone figure thirty thousand years old, with her pendulous breasts, outsized buttocks, and plaited hair.

Abstracted images with Venus inscriptions of the female body. Worn as pendants, placed in graves, and sculptured from polished clay and mammoth ivory. Rendered part bird, part snake, holding a crescent moon, a child, or phallus, these earliest representations of the female nude linger in collective pre-consciousness. And the statue remains in place and her face stares at me, the herbs and leaves blow in from the beach, the tears of fifty years splash down on my face, and the lips go on speaking. Few people hear this.

Se di diletto la tua mente pasce.

(If on delight your mind should feed)

Who is this woman? Mané asks.

A woman who gratifies herself with sensual pleasures.

What are the most requisite qualities for her to possess?

Metamorphosis.

What do you mean by that?

I mean that to give herself up to lascivious pleasure, she should be like Proteus of ancient times, able to assume every form and to know the ways of pleasuring, the finesse of her sex.

Let's talk about your past. What school did you attend?

The University of V.

What is V?

Venus. Of Venus?

I have not heard of such a learning place.

Was it coed?

No a one sex private institution.

Can you explain?

A sexual initiation to womanhood.

   One girl educates the other in the nature of love: physiology, sexual techniques and the differing psychology of man and woman, various degrees of physical beauty....I guess you could say it was girl talk.

And after that did you receive a higher education?

Since you loved me, I know what is good.

So you are saying I measured up to your expectations.

Precisely that. I couldn't put it in a better way.

Parental guidance?

I find all my mothers' stories were just to frighten me off sex.

Any beliefs you hold?

I believe we were created for making love, and when we begin to love we begin to live and everything we do should focus around feelings.

At first did it seem a little strange?

I will tell you the truth. You remember you told me about the pleasure and feeling of lovemaking. I can add now a great deal more of my own experience.

You mentioned a Musician. Did he write a song for you?

It's sexy, funny and it's a sad song. It ends with "I don't know what love is." I don't know what love is either, but I know what I feel when someone undresses me, especially with their eyes, and whether it is love or not is beside the point. I like what I feel.

So you'll continue to pose nude for the Artist.

Many times. Because the artist is looking, I am actually being a nude, a figure of a woman presented for pleasure, men go to war over it, women sacrifice themselves to its worship. Perhaps I am obsessed by it. I think an Artist is too.

In the human desire for sensuality, her body becomes a site where the flowering occurs. She showed him her bureau, she opened the drawer. Revealing her flowers of perfection, at once silken underwear, soft briefs, all women's intimates, sanctified by delicate perfume. Flowers of every color, lacy and embroidered. From violet to fuchsia, petals from every shade of damask rose to oriental orchid, from satin reds to tulip blacks, from hyacinth blues to gardenia white. The entire topiary of female concupiscence put together by a woman who had obviously wore the items for her own sensual pleasure.

They are my privacy.

They are my documents.

You can have one.

Touched by the inventory of human sexuality, Mané smoothed it out with care and wrote her name and his on the silky surface, folded it briefly and put it in his pocket.

Is an artist a voyeur?

The relationship of the artist looking at his model naked is one which allows the viewer to see truth of their existence of desires in art, or, through art, as your physical body emanates desires. From this short critique, Dumas uses voyeurism, the act of one person looking at another- to draw the viewer's attention to the source of desire. The way of all flesh has paved the way for all art where nudes are meant to seduce the eye. Yet Untitled Voyeur (1982) is the most erotic picture and does not have a body in it unless you count the slightly parted halves of red as a body.

This picture, the Artist said, has less to do with what is, than with the sense of desire it evokes, the desire to see, found in every act of trespass. The sexuality of vision... looking at things that are looking back at you. What is revealed through drawings, beautiful episodes, you use all these butterflies of intimacy, all the female tricks of attracting a man's attention... eyes looking softly at me, your legs exposed, or deliberately covered. The image you give as woman ...I am forced to say yes or no.

What else do you do in this lonely city?

I'll tell you a secret. I have undressed in front of the window, seven stories high and a man watched me with his telescope aimed at my arse. If the room were darker, he'd see my desire. I have done all this, I have done none of this, and I am my mother's daughter.

38

Then my hands invent another body for your body, lying like a fallen angel in the morning, in the evening: kiss a man on a mouth. The habits of kiss, to touch or caress the lips as a sign of greeting or leaving, to meet or touch lightly. A light meeting or touch. Kiss me there, where I am round or ripened fruit. Kiss me wherever I shudder.

II

We were alone, but not alone as one who shuts the door and feels loneliness. From the window you could see the city, from below came the scent of wild freesias. And there was the much-used bed, with its worn out mattress. It held the bodies of each clandestine act, but only the ecstasy from one Lover, and even when she remembers after so many years in the house, she is with Mané again. Divine portals of paintings, how she was painted in flesh, paint grayness through cigarette smoke, paint clarity through ice in a glass, the way an Artist painted her.

I feel like I am painting an angel, she feels mobile but mon angel … if I do this again, let me itemize this, through the chromium and eggshell whiteness, tempura with breast, belly, thighs, a transparent description of abundance of flesh, time with you (at a cost like this) it includes a warm interior; there are no boundaries inside herself.

She is being what an artist wants. When she breathes, note everything before she ever breathed, when you met her before, and in that painting, the brush remembers from different room, a shape of woman circled by her fire. He touched her shadow and she stayed… she came towards him, to slide down the sweated sheet. You can have an angel if you buy one, she said. Still, the Artist wonders if he is the first, if there has been no one else. As he detects the taste of violet on her tongue, he knew he counted for the smallest grain of balance.

She lets anyone into her room. She lets the Artist stand behind an oriental screen (one may make wood thin grained) boards which appear wet, like watered silks). He takes out a small book from his pocket; he looks into the room and begins to sketch her.

40

You call her beautiful again and celebrate. And by the end of the night, it is what she loves: the mixed-up smell of this bed, intimate spaces of double things. Each new contract is open to you when she is free from the ties of the man before you. For sexual favors, for dollars on the table. This room, this bed, this mattress. Nothing fits, nothing is planned, everything is arranged, bought from flea markets. Everything here is used. A single wardrobe and a chair covered with faded blue velvet.

For all the men in her dim cubicle tonight, with memories of forever, on mingled scent of musk and glistening oil, that palpitating sound and smell, damp hair, mine. I do not know whose hands they are. What lists of tricks, flirtations mastered, lists of what a woman has learned to do with a man: slowing him down, the hands explore her shape he has to guess at, he touches her with the heat of fingertips.

When you have the time, I'll draw you with willow or charcoal, the Artist said. The alchemy of this body with your body, show you, chez fallen angel, what you do to give yourself time, what metallurgy happens as sound of rusted bedsprings, trapped in that sweet ambush. You give out such healing that the time of Saints is come back and dead men rise, damn yourself, pure idol, innocent gift, laugh, sigh, and die for love.

Figmental drawing of a woman on the wall. He had kept the drawing of the woman. For what? Suddenly I started to translate the drawing into poems. I was held by a gust of thoughts, and I covered his drawing in words. The relationship between artist and woman, is the passion of the woman in his bed. Be female to this male, her Muse — kiss your conqueror. Count the women in this life. Like money... statue girl, in a rut, act crazy, mistress of flesh, Lover be more, be more savage, and more holy, this is the place.

The thought burned with warmest intensity as if someone had opened the door and released a thousand fireflies in the darkened

41

room. When does a man become a woman's possession? When she is a Lover... a Girlfriend...a Wife? If one possesses such a man securely. Does she uses him like a habit when the man holds her. And what does it matter. She is a woman and a woman needs things that she can use, *love nakedly, you are wilder than the night. I am suffering from promiscuity and obscurity.* Habits of sex reveal who we are, the phenomena or activity of life concerned with sexual desire, informal sexual gratification.

I did not work for a living.

You kept me. Lover, secretly behind your smile.

In this astrology of sex, this fertile month, who touches you tonight? You found unbelievable contrasts of innocence; your necklace is the last lonely light, seeing that girl yesterday, innocence, the swish of pages you try to write thick formulations, on old red paper, crepe de chine, the sound as the dress slipped off your shoulder.

The light is low in the sky and as dusk falls, it fills the room with tangerine light that traces a perfect shadow of the ghost palm on the inner wall. Touch her. And he does. So many times. A prime woman, an abandoned woman; perhaps originally a passionate one, he is lying with a woman that has just lain with another man. Hot sun, cool fire tempered with seductive words, black shade, shine sun, burn fire, breathe air and play with me. The private parts of a woman in the field of Venus. We make a toy of love. Forged primitive in the shape of a man. Each one of us is wounded. It must be so. Some nights, I feel comfort under a paunched stranger's belly.

III

Describe it in rooms hidden above the street. In such rooms, shadows of men, stripped past the ribcage, come and go. Her soft bed; the heavy purple throw and over them spread thick blankets and a robe she wraps round and round her body in soft red silk. These delicate thoughts reminds me of how easy it has been; for what else do we hold now than a woman's softness against the hardness of him. From hard armor to soft robes, the two connected by the orbit of the rushing night, while pen and paper and sable brushes retracing hundreds of curves and lines, upwards and downwards and between, as if a hand moves to touch her, you held a tiny magnet inside a ring engraved with poetry, and you listed first things...what was imagined... I saw you across arcs of moon, I saw you falling through the stars, a controlled fall beyond the usual hold you had of yourself.

Men are such exquisite hell. When the men say they love you, it's like loosing your balance, always slipping into this sexual collaboration and what sweet thing they do to you, there is a right side for the feeling and unfolding, something warm in the holding, lethal addiction, nymphomaniac, when I'm sick of this business, some kink in my nature brings me back, dollar bills that's how desire catches me, from morning to night, what about sleep, turn over. Or take all of me, but don't take care of me, celebrate champagne and chilled wine, to take me slightly drunk. Squeeze me into every other afternoon between your wife and girlfriend. Don't say. Sleepwalking into the solemn years, your dark eyes more fluent than the green ones, though nothing matters. From you, you have taken night, framing it to sex, maybe a little atonement.

Why do you like women?

For one thing, that you are my woman.

Women are the best creatures in the world.

Next to men and bees.

As honey.

I have never before known what you were and how you have
made me so I don't know who I am myself, I only know that I must
endure intolerable passions for unknown pleasures. I hear you
breathing next to me. For the breath, it is said to be changed according to passions of the body or according to its own passions. Held to
the passions of the body, I am x-rated, beautifully adulterated, by
you. Yet, like a thick pulse that has not been broken. I do not deceive
myself that it is not the same. No, it has always been that way. Even
as you tell me love while half asleep. In the light hours of the room.
I have already heard you. And then you fall back to sleep, my pillow
pressed against lightly against your cheek, your face, beautiful. I could
see echoes of a face seen in the past by other lovers. How her kisses
might have touched. Your face... the man I know, the first vision of
you in an angel's mask, as I would see it again. I looked in his eyes. I
am no thought-catcher, but I guess you are sad.

What do you think of love?

More than I think of hate.

And why?

Because it is better to hate the things that you love, than to love
the things that at times make you hate. With other women, it comes
from the mouth... like blowing winds, which rustle the leaves and yet
can uproot the trees in a blow; or fire which warms at a distance and

44

burns close up, igniting everything; or the sea, which makes the sail calm or sinks boats in a storm. To stand away from love, nature and lightning as it strikes, in a thousand shivers, most things break us without warning.

Much of life is about calculations. To count time on lines of your palm, from roots to fronds. How could time and earth's history stretch on a one-dimensional line, from beginning to the end. Mathematical rules that find answers, draw conclusions. For instance, the answer to the magnate equation: what is the ratio of fertile women and men in this city? How much sex, on average in a month, how long will this relationship last. I did not calculate anything lasting longer than the limit of his hand. Intimacy needs no measuring to exist. So he showed me. A man who works with his hands holds the key. Later we had sex among the fossils.

What images return?

Faded paint. Fractured windows like old bones. The images trailing through doorways. Appearing and disappearing, images transferred among fish and ink and white sheets crumpled by this biology, this intimate theology. Our room as a cave at night, a tent in sunlight, a Baroque pavilion late afternoon. The sexual shadows, friction and passion. Then your body arching in the curtains ravine, red silk enflaming, my skin.

Looking at you, the moment's surrender, I can see you... softly denuded exact shaping of shadow. Following every curve of you., the Artist said.

Turning inwards, we have dreamed these things in our deepest lives and they are ourselves. And all this time, I have shared your room as if I am the only lover who has ever had you. I came here on my own and have been sleeping there under your earth. And room by room, touch by touch. Earth smells of aftershave anointment, all the things you touched with your hands, and moss you left with all the bedroom musk, as it exists with all the night and afternoon heat.

She makes him feel so loved that he can hardly stop himself from leaving. To see him come out of a brothel ? Is there shame? It was no shame to go out, but a shame to go in, the Artist said. For ourselves again we are like torches of wax, like candles lighted in the hallway, of which you may make doves or vultures, roses or nettles, laurel or elder for disgrace...the disgraced tree because one man hung himself on a branch of it. But then who will tell. This midnight sex was real.

IV

In a white painted room is full of titanium crystals, so many of them airborne, they drifted from the white painted walls onto her body and landed on her skin but your drawings fit into this room. A hundred strokes he draws and then stops and starts again. In the drawing, she is wearing a white silk slip with nothing underneath. Who lifted up her dress, (she said). But the material is only thin as cloth lets him know, the Artist can see through the fabric, the triangle of her own black delta, the half-opened thighs spread and give way to his lines.

Turning her face to meet this man with her invisible perfume, now she bends over. And the Artist sees a thin strap at the top of the slip, catching it in his eyes as it falls off her shoulder. Immeasurable white silk falling down and exposing half her breast, so near to her heart it lays, the brown halo around her nipples. I was what you would brush with your palm. What your fingers would touch. It was you, on my right, on my left. It was you by that white window's billowing silk moiré, who moved to disengage his gaze trapped between her breasts. A voice calling you back. And you as Surrealist laid paint against her white. Silk.

Practically blind, you gave him sight and the shadows heightened it. Her lips parted, he rendered the mouth in tender trace using the tip of a brush, to work in its whorls, his outlines were precision, as emotional and delicately anatomical. A tender brushing of warmest magenta spreading like pink ink on her skin. Spreading and spreading. Who makes the color. The red candle was real. The valley of her belly.

Who knows her?

Everything in her room was warm and real. She shows him things he has not known. Where to touch her, dare to pleasure her. She revealed orgasmic secrets without markers, enclosed secrets and exposed secrets to him during the night, as if she was from an ancient tribe, no longer scared that photographs will take her soul away. His lips on her mouth makes her moan, makes the earth moan. The magma in the spine and all bones melt. I have drawn the glistening seeds, who finds this girl first and makes her a woman. If she shut both eyes and breathe in his heat... deep laid nerves like secret maps for deep-laid routes, she shows me the way into her body, enters her, for its own reasons & her loose hair falling, the revered anatomy of this bone, and how it fuses inside when her muscles, friction are pilot less, her own speed made from one emotion, crimson, one intense diffusion.

I knew the diverse tastes this man. Knew the smells of musk and sandalwood from your skin, and your deep male voice, those testosterone notes, hung in the room, as tympani.

You left the next morning, but you left without saying good-bye. I missed you. I missed the sound of your voice Leaving was your own choice, bed, woman, the living blood inside her. You were lost to me after that. I put out my hand and felt only a warm mattress, a warm absence where you had been.

Was your heart arrowed with loss, even before I met you?

I would lay my head on your heart, a heart beating with its river, deep within your side. It was wounded by love. I heard it bleed.

Have I changed much, Mané ?

If the Lover is there cannot be any Lover accept you and there is no change that can happen (and make you not my lover).Some changes occur in the room... the woman is still the same. Staring at the cherub-haunted ceiling. For nothing is left to be told unless it has been told by an angel, the Artist said.

What do they tell you to do? Do they tell you to love me?

They didn't tell me that. But I do, I love you more than I used to.

Dumas's reclining figures, male and female look out at us directly out of the paper. There is no background except for a single monochrome color, so the figures could be anywhere.

I did not understand another mystery, the Artist said. But that night when we were in bed together, I stayed awake all night, warm as an animal with you beside me, like a warm pool, then night folds over me, black, black like the dark lines on my drawing multiplied. I thought about the men of various colorings visited your bed, its velvet leaving no record but the spasm of muscle. I have never asked or questioned this intimacy between us, it happened from the beginning.

I allow these images, the Artist said, you are beautiful, with looks of arch and indent, still, from other sleepless lovers. Then what you did when you undressed as a concubine, unhook the dress, sweet disorder of lace, here, is perfect. It does this: keeps you moist like a fertile flower. Wildly scented. So sexual it is felt. You with your head pressed in the feather pillow, held in the sacred rites of sleep, while I lay awake and pushing a hundred black sheep over the stile, so hard, so many dark animals in the dark, I could not count them all, but when I lie awake, I can't get sleepless animals out of my mind.

Did you think about me?

Mané, I missed you when you left. I did not forget you, but forgot the number of times I made love to others. I forget birthdays, even the names of friends, but nothing can make me forget the number of the house. The number 56 is still in my mind where I engraved it years ago. I resumed my life in other locations. I decided to become reckless, so I wouldn't drag life out for too long.

I lived out my life, work, money, and talk - I was not tied to the world. I did not belong to the real world. I was not afraid to die. I lived in the realm of intoxication, in which I include ice in a glass and tiny paper umbrellas stuck into maraschino cherry, nothing durable: I worked at Flora's on South Park, The Gentlemen's Club, White Mansion at the top of Cuba Street.; working to alchemize a life in the future. The sad thing is, if you had stayed one more night. I would have left with you. I would catch up with the woman I wanted to be.

What of the room in the first brothel, the perfume of freesia flowers, the white house at 56? The garden too.

They will tear it down. The simplest white: doors and petals. The simplest fate: demolition and oblivion.

His drawings in the late 1980's are filled with detailed observations, nothing is as it might first appear, nothing is ever stable. Yet even in this personal world, there remain hints of its surreal nature, a feeling of lost women waiting between nights. There are also secrets waiting to be discovered. They are Mané's details and one has to look for clues in each painting to reveal the depth of his evocative narrative.

At the center of one painting is an anonymous reclining woman, her eyes closed, one hand on her right breast, her left hand placed suggestively between her legs.

The room in which he places her, is filled with symbols in the present and the past, the whole painting is a metaphor. She looks away from us. Dumas has caught the woman in a private moment. There is a strong sensuality in the painting. Sex and sexual liaisons are central to Mané's other works. In the collection Human Rhythms, Dumas has encompassed the principles of two modes of life force in this composition. With the masculine yang and the feminine yin, Coming Together (1984) depicts the fabric of nature and elicit affairs, with its changing relationships, through the weave of attracted forces on the paintings surface: a fully clothed man enters the door of the room, and a naked woman poses against a see-through curtain in patterned lace, the vigorous black lines, rich in sexuality and yet scared of intimacy.

PART III

I

I meet the Artist. By chance.

Nothing in the world happens by chance, Mané said. Chance becomes the spaces between the shifting arrows of time. Chances are that the arrow moves towards a fixed point is nothing but an impulse received from the archer. Whatever is natural reaches its end by its own accord. This endless genesis. Organic jungle of another.

I daydream such images, small fragments of silk, tissue paper and if you could move my thoughts like the grasses or pull them apart like the wings of a butterfly, one by one... there is a story attached to each fabric, each word on each fragment of paper. It is our story Lover. And in some parts, it is true. And one does not teach the other this, for the force of desire is so strong and yet these naked couplets are gentle and keep me from dissolving.

But somewhere on a journey, you meet another traveling in the same direction. (In the passage, the text only establishes where she was for one night and it is based on first-hand knowledge, it proves her stay alone was interrupted but does not go into detail). They neglected to give witness to the exact hour the man entered the house or left. I think that a stranger can remind you of another lover, when you meet for the first time. A force drives you. The desire to re-create something that existed. It is the passion to give form to your deepest feelings, your deepest longings, your dreams – who you are. The link between you and

51

something outside yourself that enlarges your world. You changed the way I feel, you changed how I see. When my thigh accidentally touches your thigh, on a train, on a bus, on a plane. Letting impulses and feelings free. A man's clairvoyant voice, his green eyes behind dark glasses. I had a vision of you since childhood, but only remembered you now. And I share a taxi to your hotel room.

II

She met a man who spoke Spanish. Talked about scraps of things in gypsy words… Pieces of gold, doves/sheets, moon/a shirt, a thief/those who steal at dusk, guns/candles.. This man (smile) how good it was to make conversation… commandments/the fingers, Saint asleep/to rob a person asleep, lanterns/eyes, a spy, and dancing/to take flight…

The baptism of thought, he said, the thought blessed, by their sound the birds frighten and depart and the winds and words scatter us. I live in a country, the language I do not understand: It will defeat itself. It has outlived its songbirds The bamboo bird cage also. The emptiness will ruin us. It will bring the house down.

If you could you see the house, his door opens.. A bed, a desk. And in the realm of a house, his papers are folded like a flock of birds, from room to room. As many birds in cages and white peacocks on green lawn. Until a woman said, kill all birds, except birds with white feathers, in no other explanation.

Of all our assassinations which are natural for us, he said, it is done with the hand, by converting fingers into tongues words unspoken are entered, as the birds' ethereal flight after silver knife cut a throat, as many words as the transcriber writes so many wounds the birds receive. A flock may be saved by the calligraphers and chrysographers, transcribers and illuminators of manuscripts.

Poet you are born with a mouthful of birds. The doves against the new moon. It is to bring back the birds back; it is to bring back this man (kiss). To re-enter your text. Soft emerald eyes... Consider this color of the eye as beautiful and the Spanish celebrate it in song as the Villancico:

Ay los mis ojuelos,

Ay hagan los cielos

Tengo confianza

De mis verdes ojos.

Que de mi te acuerdes.

Dante speaks of her eyes as emeralds: Purgatorio, xxxi. I note she has no necklace, nothing but bare skin at her throat. I can, says Lami in his Annotazioni, "Erano I suoi occhi d'un turchino verdiccio, simile a quel del mare." Talked about scraps of things in gypsy words...until the touch of his lips is felt even after he has gone.

When he knows you he will love you, *your eyes are the same color green as mine,* to speak *ay ojuelos verdes* with the one who catches your smile, leaves me with a desire for him to touch me. And it feels like we have already kissed (but I did not ask your name... the sound of your voice makes it all right) to walk back with the one you meet; roads that move, they carry us where we want to go, between us and heaven and hell there is only love and sex. Being alive, our cells remind us; we are masters of our own acts. This is what a woman believes. It is human and it is real; one feels it; all living cells, all the parts of one's own self.

III

I sensed you before I saw you. It was a feeling that touched me as if it were a hand, the Artist said. Then the train stops at the station of a rural town. I think it was the town was Cahors. And a beautiful woman enters the carriage and looks around, sees the empty seat next to the man.

She was just like him, alone, in need of a lover.

A man turned around to see the woman in the railway carriage. When she lifts a bag on a shelf, he will see more. As his eyes trace skin. Her secret boundary of exposure between her blue jeans and white shirt a field of blue lavender. In the change of white, he senses a quiver of red silk and lace. It is in this pulse sent from her; the Lover will translate inside himself. Aware of the scent of a stranger that distinguishes her from other women of the earth, you can detect musk on moistened skin, the warm animal of her. And if you touch me you will change me, for touch and change occur in the same moment.

Then the train pulls out of the station. Then she becomes aware of the heat of the man, the rhythm of the train and the man as he presses against her. She does not try to move away from him. In slow motion, he moves his hand on the seat between his thigh and hers and then she feels his hand slipping under her thigh.

She stares out the window. On both sides of the track rows of sunflowers appeared as far as the eye could see; those yellow petals which betray summer. She stares at the flowers as if she has never seen sunflowers before, imagining the symmetry & whirling pattern of seed, a way of interpreting the sexual meaning with our lips. Anyone's lips? The Van Gogh yellow discs like drying sun and a flight of pink feathered birds (wild pigeon), as they landed amongst the flowers. Then the train pulls out of another station, I think it was Toulouse. The train moves on two rails bent by force into a curve, the direction of the line, which it desires to return. Then his fingers are parting her thighs and they are sliding between her legs, pulling the lace to one side.

The train enters a tunnel; I think the tunnel that crosses over the Lot River close to the medieval town with the bridge that was washed away in seasonal rains. There is the rocking of the train, the dark tunnel, the long hard whistle of the train as the long train pulls through. The woman was looking off into the fields. They were yellow in the sunset. The sun sets in blood red clouds. Then he heard her speak.

They look like fire, she said.

I work with fire.

What is your work?

Iron, fire, he said.

I do not understand.

He makes a play with his hands of someone holding charcoal.

So you are an artist.

He smiles.

I know so little of you, Mané said. I would like to know more.

And so I began to know the sound of your voice, fragile filigree of unspoken words as an invisible sound that has no beginning or end. Infinite merger. All this I am. The curve of your body was sensual architecture seen in recent dreams. Mané gets up and approaches her. Pulls her to her feet as if he is asking her to dance.

I want to hold you.

I want to say things to you now that are never said.

There is not much time, she said.

Once a season, the farmers have a ritual. They burn old flowers, in the fields, in a bonfire; whatever is not alive, they burn. The woman looked out of the apocalypse of burning sunflowers, the sky on fire, and then she looked into his face. Younger, suntanned. The hands of the young artist on her hips. The heat of his body passing as human warmth through her thin cotton dress.

I feel like we are on the other side, she said.

This metamorphous waited.

IV

He starts to love her as the fragments enter. He reads her code as if she has a tattoo on her soul, so he could find her through all time, when the sun has set, when the moon has set, and the last human fire has gone out, he will find her like a shadow under his heart. There was, in those words an unspoken code deciphered between words he was asking her lips, her eyes, her body if she would bear his children, and stay with him... if she had always be his lover. What holds you at gunpoint, she said, how fragile the celebrations are.

All things imperfect, impermanent and incomplete. It's a question of how much we need. There have been times; I never asked what a man wanted. I knew what you saw in me by the way I make you look, for yes, you will never forget the first moment I took off my clothes and my thigh at the crossing. Remember when you spoke of black ink, of breath into an image, a thought, waiting for one brush stroke, your stroke. The alchemy blends into this.

Mané slowly begins to unlace her. (So you let him) .The symmetry of laces on leather boots, you had just undone the first knot, when I found you kissing my inner thigh, and each one he releases the tension in his fingers tightens, he feels an attraction that seems to claim all the blood in his body.

After days and nights of being with you, we become our own dreams, weightless and rare. As I see them, they are an arrangement of paper cut into a rectangle (9 inches by 6 inches) and bound at the seams as if they are about to fly, by a breath of wind, but I opened my hand and held a portion of the words in my fist- what can I tell you... I had dreams about the Artist. With him, I might have traveled the world, from city to city, knowing the women he drew, framing his paintings with my own hands.

V

For the winter, Mané rented a house, 12,000 feet in the Colorado mountains. The windows shuttered & latticed, creating shadows on the snow. At first, he liked staying in the atmosphere, the rooms of dusty medicinal almanacs and history books, the skin of a zebra in front of the fire, the statue of a woman in flowing robes, holding a clock with a swinging pendulum in her right hand. But soon he had to hide the anonymous certificate of marriage hanging in the hall, its flowering vines dry and faded. He collected the shoes and jackets from the deer antler stand, the miniature spoons and porcelain dogs, the sepia photograph of a uniformed soldier, and hid them in a cupboard.

He liked the claw foot bath in the attic room, the fractured glass from bullet holes in the window of the living room, the streetlight cocooned in fog. He stood watching the snow falling over the white streets. The emotion roused by the whiteness, the silence of it.

The altitude high, the air white and cold, almost blue. How well he drew in that room. The fire burning every day, whole storms were left out. And hot chocolate in thick china cups. And the atmosphere grew warmer ,richer, the chocolate itself.

In the drawing, the same woman is on the bed. She is lying on the goose-feather quilt embossed with lovers' initials & good luck charms, for mystery, for the unknown; in-between all the pillows, her hips raised towards him, fitting closely to the joints, the left knee bent up in a movement, her bare foot disappears into a fold of sheet, transparent & thin, with folds unbroken, clinging close to the soul of her feet, soft lights with opaque reflection, shadow-less close-up, a hand encircling embroidered conformity on the hem end falling upwards, with movement, separated by fingers and according to the folds, her right arm behind frames her head, and in the drawing, her hair is falling over her right shoulder exposing her throat.

58

PART IV

I

Bound in full mottled calf, hinges expertly and most invisibly repaired. Spine with six raised beds and red morocco gilt lettering on the label, the edges sprinkled with red (ink) at an early date in a vellum leaf from a choir book, initials and decorations in red, stones ruled in red. Yapp edges. The roots are telling.

Many images are transparent passing through my mind like drawings on paper surfaces. *A Room in the Villa* (1980) *Woman Etched in Aqua* (1978) *Interior of the Hotel Room* (1990) *Woman Seated in Profile* (1998)*Interior with child* (1981), *Interior, Train Carriage* (2001), *Interior: Flowers and Cats* (1992)*In the Interior* (2005) content of drawings and in their framing of time: a drawings essential feature is its image on a wall.

This sensory nemesis, *pictura poesis* you do it well, (a shoulder, a hip) the life of the senses, of art, according to the artisan, you create an art object according to your hands, each image makes itself believable with this realistic texture; yet I do not mistake it for reality, even though in some drawings the two dimential, the two of us, of me and here I am, and there I am on our bed posing for the image… it makes me passionate, just to lie there on the quilt, with the wood burning in the fire, the clarity it gives to red wine, the crystal shining, the reserve of red, fiery and deep.

And then from this a feeling begins because one hand touches him. And this: that we lie down and then we are, on a bed. And this: that burning into this body, if someone opens the door Lover… pull the sheet over, our eyelids closing… bodies still… as

59

if sleeping... an opulent mattress in an extravagant room at the grand hotel by the Italian lake. Mané and I sleep and wake in palaces, Egyptian cotton sheeting with a thousand thread count and monogrammed initials, exquisite white space, I drank your saliva, I pulled the sky across your shoulders. One long summer, we felt heat in our mouths, then talked among the crowding leaves of lemon verbena trees, so much to say, words evaporate into thick air, these thoughts reached you. And this was done. We were never detached (and so the work, she wrote, in part, will be deserving of censure).

The continued existence of (the woman) of her body; the head moving (her thoughts solid) confirms the existence of my face as it is portrayed by you. Any imagined image (skin, thigh, a woman's face) is exposed by ways in which light exposes the structure of the artist's world- slant, reflection, color, illumination. Like wheat left out in the sun. And here the page is, the ghost palm shadows move along the paper, the dark ink running across the page, when the surface of the inky paper is a face, eyes like sharp desire. I saw beyond the inky river... the pen sprang up like a branch in your hand. Soon the tracing will be done.

You take as much care over each contour, you take days and weeks, as if my body was to be copied on a frieze in a Palace wall: copied as a beautiful relief on chalky facades long ago, luscious gardens, zinc flowers and genesis of erotica. Or an outline of Cleopatra after Anthony came or Mona Lisa as her smile. Time does not alter chalk or lime. They remain transparent. In the picture, you construct me, like a beautiful object, an image of female shadows cast on a blanc wall, a woman standing in front of white drapes, the effect of the white is dazzling, but as you fix your eye on the painting, two pools of color start to emerge from the canvas, as if they are two separate waters from the lake of a book.

First, there is the woman. And in the background, darkness and shadows of the interior. A man holds that image like breath, long enough to see more than her outline, or shoreline before first light. It is continuous shadow; and the way you see her similarity to the casting of other women, the Artist is careful to place the sheen of light on the surface to make it perfect, an artist understands shadowing, he knows light cannot pass through her body, from natural forces although a man is a counterpoint the deep structure of reproducing her beautiful image.

II

His body is silhouetted against the night. From closer in, a shiver in his body is answered by her, as she presses her hips against him. He lets go his breath in a sudden rush when he comes. The River. She saw his floating heart. The witness. She has seen him bleed. This woman at the end, The stranger. The one he configures love for. The mathematician. She knew the things that counted for happiness. The whore. She took the seed of all and the glistening core of him. The Shrine. Of all her bones and what is in her soul. The woman. The real one. Closer to her, he surfaces.

Mané, now we only have ourselves to give. In the arms of a lover, made real by the act of love. Desire for the desire. It did not matter where. I love, for love is made real in the act of loving you. To give each other our lips, and then a kiss. And after, like ghosts and saints, we are answered by our own voices that move like a lantern through the room. *Dialogue of Drawing. (1978)*

Let me borrow your pencil, I will draw and you will see.

Here.

The lead breaks.

You push too hard.

Think of the weight of black on a floating piece of paper, or a strand of hair as a soft line along a neck. A line is not difficult but it has a fate unless you let it float. But the motion takes place without you forcing it. You can't fake it.

I cannot draw.

Your eye does not follow your hand.

Now it is worse.

Your hand does not follow your mind. Your eye and your mind must all draw together.

I would rather make love to you than draw on this paper. But how have I done here?

You draw roses and kisses shadowed with prayers and promises. Vows irrevocable. The ones that slipped out of your mouth before. I hold your body to it. You have been loved by many, I know it, though you will not admit it, you whose body is insatiable and like an unquenchable lust. Velvet is on your bones. It rubs off on mine.

I smiled. Is drawing like carving?

Like an impulse received from stone.

Your hand is the reason the mountains quake when your chisel moves. The vanity of stone.

Is there a pattern or rhythm your fingers move too?

The only pattern I could conceive was you, while dreaming asleep. Like a sleeper who turns in his sleep, and as he moves, he moves the sheet before him with his hand. Stone carving. I carved things deep and hollow, sad thoughts shaken with fever, old wounds, a life without you, then with you, slow, pulse recognition.

I watched your hands open the fingers of the angel nailed to the clouds. You made her cry. And the sound came to me: the sound of loss. I was wondering if you heard. First the losing, then leaving. As if tiny losses added up to the final loss. Prepared her for leaving you. I cannot say this word easily. Death. For death. A dying. You turned her skin into ivory with chisels, almost, but not quite, to touch the shadow of a ghost possessed by your hands. You do not loose touch.

Undressing before the mirror, where he could see her, (*many nudes, whole figures*) she let everything fall way, fall to the floor, then naked, firm muscles showing under her skin, *(arms, legs, feet and positions)* the round curve of her hips, her soft skin, the line of her torso. A fine line the artist drew rounded at the shoulder and butt, ran from elbow to foot, the tender line, the sweep of flesh, the shine of silk.

Will we ever fade from exposure?

Deep hollows shading her sex, reminded him of an animal, an animal with a scent that intoxicated the world. The Artist stared, his pencil balanced between the index finger and thumb of his right hand. Obsessed, possessed as she made him and then he closed his eyes so he could not see her in the room; he found the animal appeared in the darkness behind him, it would stay there behind his eyes as part of his body forever.

For the more I knew you, the more I loved you, I loved you until I was too much in love with you, Mané said.

I felt the same.

Do you think I should not fall too much in love with you? He asked.

That depends. If in the falling, you loose yourself.

But then, I see some secrets written on your brow but they are not yet written in your eyes. The look you give me (The face of Madonna, ascending into heaven).

Is it a question?

I have no idea, in the end, whether I will still love you,

But I want to stay with you, to see whether this is true.

You reach the part where you are in a fevered dream, Lover, we do not stand up to do the following things, not a slow dance, but more , like a salsa or tango where your hips grinding into mine. And parts of our body- and our hands and fingers... I hold what you hold- it feels warm in places (how he takes her and how she receives him-the act of giving). He goes down to a room of scent, he has been there before, to pick out from among the fragrance, the one most richly hers. From the bedroom window, hung a blue shirt. Smells of musk mingled with perfume. It feels like something of yours I wear.

It feels like a love shirt.

But this was no accidental color. The Artist had seen it before, so he draws her between blue of atmosphere, between the green of her eye and blue of intensity in the veins in the thicket & wild (hedges). Vegetation is the surface on which motion takes place, thrusting sprays (of roses), the white spill (of paint) you may have cause to censure me for saying this: but Mané has positioned her. The God of women for the artist.

III

So we remember the long plastered ceilings, and back into words that we spoke, the dust of past and present, joined at the seams without any separations, like faces in faded photographs looking back out of an old frame, whose metaphor was forgotten, but then you begin to understand the power of the image as if you always knew so much.

The painted bed forms a renaissance painting behind her. The Artist arranged pomegranates, cornflowers, wild poppies & lilies on the table; contemplated how all that is opaque, is tinged by the object next to it. The lilies colored in diver's colors, all seem reflected in the open air, without shadow, then white canvas and the wall facing. He listened to the model breathing through the white; he saw her eyes close, for she was the only sleeper in that white canvas.

She being a beautiful woman. Clarity to breasts, thighs, lips, together, a drawing, the Artist thought, sexy imagery remains for an afternoon, as taken as stolen when you looked through the window frame, with red freesias on the sill, summer light soaks orange citrus cast, deeply, whole afternoon, framing harlequin grill.

One sable brush stroke he would make, over her whole beautiful length, he could paint how he sees her, since his painting embraces all forms of her: and he frames what he sees, a face exquisitely turned, the parting of lips on double red divide. He keeps framing the woman, in his head, in his mind, looking at light and shadows tracing back to some primitive cosmology of cave drawing, where each drawing has to do with natural form; if one describes deep chasms and earths own fire; what effect heat has on a body.

He wanted to make love to her again, among heat, flute& bird-song. When he finished, the flowers on the table, the fruit split pink of its own ripeness, he gave her a spoon but no bowl. and drops of juice could be heard falling one by one through the taut moiré. The sheets were glistening with juice and seed.

You can not predict the exact route your fingers, the way you touch me there, uncovering and covering in the middle of nowhere, who cares and for all the night passions in your room, you are musk, the smell of a woman fills your bedroom, what you kiss and what I kiss for you, melts and by the time morning light enters the room, with all the heat & marrow, the middle is sweeter , when your eyes open and I ask you to say your name, I know you, my eyes see you, makes me love you. Except now we are no longer strangers.

I know your voice like timbre stone, from earlier when you tele-phoned from the city. It is an open secret between us. I whisper it out loud to myself: I did not miss you until I met you. Then suddenly seduced by the intricacies of you, as tiny intimacy as fragments that hang together, as intimate architecture, surveyed spaces inside. In the beginning, in the patterning, as love running its full trajectory. Between artifact and reality, (it is beautiful). And so it is.

You remain with me for a long time, by the passions of my body, of carnal desires, according to my own passions as desiring. Thoughts strung like a chain of pearls. Your eyes I know eclipsed on your face. Lifting my mind above, when you touch me with your thoughts. I look into your eyes. I want to tell your beautiful face to hide from growing older. Sometimes, Mané, I think you read my words.

I know the open-lips emotion she reveals and the diamond-sounds as a pen scratches paper. She is carving her own face. Virgin? Stranger? Lover? She was all these and none of them. In the biology of the blood, she was like every woman, everything that the mind of a man imagines. She had been there forever and she has never existed. Between such animal and human heat, what is intimacy? – Is it the impulse to make someone else complete? I can tell you, we live beyond our outer skin. Under these skins, there was only another woman, every woman. What did they matter the lies she told me, deceptions, in comparison with this truth. The body is the way it is, this love she has always had, from the beginning and before when I loved her in all her moments. I loved her for her belief, not for her sense of truth. I had forgotten life without her. But here, I am reminded of my emotions tearing at the heart of the book with my fingers, like fresh bread. Will she satisfy him with words; the way an artist does with just a brush and color (what if the fiber of her words has the same qualities of light and shade). Only she could answer.

IV

In a suitcase, I found letters from early days, *(also his box of colors)* simple things I had forgotten. The sound of ocean. The rhythm of sexual, of words of emotion. Had you forgotten. Blue sky & blue water. I hold them with my eyes closed, like prayers in my hands.

You and I lay as the sand lay and shifted, and moved as the days moved, one moves slowly into another. A body's course. As we sleep listening to the sound that waves make. Sleep shuts our eyes, now no more eyes but shining stars, crystallites reassembling water, which is always the same color as it runs. He begins to draw the dreams of us.

Later we eat pineapple, more plentiful at that time of year, then the day turns yellow, sand caught between our toes, the sun like paint on us, turns our legs golden – each surface takes on the color of whatever is set against it, a body in yellow light, tinged with sun (to learn to melt wax into lacquer). In the book of days, images of bodies which in winter was hidden , is now bare and exposed in summer and colors of things in the sun, squares and fields of colored beach towels, until we become messengers of some aromatic summer, color by color, which was never ended.

I remember the pattern and weight of these things...take seeds of sweet pineapple, one can touch a mouthful. To re-work memory (to learn to work flesh tints in tempura). For memory reworks the interludes of her mind. The sun visible in the sky and we look up to see it; and the Artist sees the sun above the sand and the sun sees us from above, for the sun looks down on us as we look up; the sun reflects in one way and but an artist sees it in a day of yellow. These fragments begin...

How much nakedness do you have left to give me?

(Take these clothes from me).We have passed so many days and nights together. How long will you undress for me? Mané asked. It is like a pile of fabric. Unhooked and folded. Then as he knows, how it hugs places on a body. As gossamer or skin. Especially the red dress as it held you inside. And my arms matched it, holding you tight. Then my fingers aching to grasp the metal behind your back and pull down the zip, to shed it. Already these images stay inside the cusp of dream.

And you?

I have a dream that repeats itself. I am lying on a thin sleeping mat made from fingers of bamboo interlocked together and I realize my body is teaching me to adapt .You are sharing the same mat. And in the true intimacy of us –sleeping on dirt floor: the simple places save us: as the grain of dirt survives if it becomes a star. Midnight and time spins away, squeezed past shadows: I felt as if I was dreaming. Tonight the feelings for you pile up inside me. You are author of how I feel. To hold and maintain this delicate point of balance... balanced like a rider, this sexual equilibrium. Like the first time to the last time. I remember it (how much can a man give a woman in one night). At some point, you become my woman, Mané said.

Engraved front piece by the historian. With a ten line poem, underneath woodcut prints on a title page decorated with initials. His inscription dated on verso of flyleaf. Another inscription recording the day he gave the book away. Among the pages, a poet can heighten emotion yet she inks the past and present. Writes ink on paper, vegetable matter set down on top of vegetable matter. Like composted thoughts, the Poet said.

How do they make ink?

A suspension of carbon from the ashes of almonds.

Anything else?

The solution of tannins from oak bark or other vegetation. To make ink, start with a renaissance recipe. Chop some wood of oak - in March or April... before they produce leaves.

Then how do they make paper?

Paper, like ink comes from vegetation. Wood (fir, pine and spruce, birch, aspen and eucalyptus); then linen, cotton, hemp, straw, reeds and grasses (reeds, elephant grass and bamboo). Egyptians wrote on papyrus, Chinese wrote on delicate grasses, wood fibers, and the silk of mulberry leaves. Because the practice of writing is a laying down of flowers on flowers, you may see it as showing someone what you are thinking. As a flowering.

Who taught you?

It was a man who taught me to use ink, rice paper and brush. He showed me the weight of water on paper, the Artist said. I was his student.

She felt the oriental brush tracing the rocks of her spine- all that belonged to the past, the delicate flick of the sable point and gentle push of water as inked pacific waves lapping on the sway of her hips, then the sand curving past the beach and a continuous line of fishing net, as it folded beneath the margins of an ocean. Words and images keep swimming into view. Images have more substance that what we dream, but less substance than what you paint.—and this- I should know it among a hundred pages—I can feel the touch of it , like sand between my fingers... it's you and I on the West Coast beach, a blanket spread on the earth. A moon-filled night, written so that the blue penguin could drift out of the mercurial blackness into the breakers. It wanted to get to its nest, for the clouds touched its feathers and, like me, it felt a storm coming. I saw it in the inward eye. Cloud upon cloud pouring down rain onto our shelter until I couldn't hear your voice for the noise of thunder. The bird cries. The images screamed behind and 'fell seething over the paper; I trapped them there. Paper (eyes moving across the word) hand (turning the pages). Small gestures with fingers lifting and turning a page; the delicate edge of the page discriminates weight of stacked pages and they must lift it away from the others. It is what makes our life different. The ink fades, fabric crumbles into pale dust; or the ghost palm overhanging the veranda catches in the shutter and clings for a moment to the wood. Everything moves back to nothing. What does it matter in the end.

V

One morning, he received a letter from the hand of a Poet, and the soul that matched it, the soul of a flat page of pen and ink and white light, red, silk, damp, torn, print or water mark, the page on the desk, wrote and spoke of kiss and take from the fold in the skin and bent knee, in the shards of love, of this groove of love, enters and grows day by day, turning up in my blood. It is warm in here. I did not ask why but gave in to it; it is better to melt the desire than wrestle with love. Cast out of the sad bed, be content to live unknown, and die undiscovered.

Later she tells him: I have been reading *In Search of Lost Time*. Did you know someone spent most of his life in bed as a grown man? His bed was a library and a desk and filled with crumbs from golden Madeline cakes scented with lemons from his garden. At times his bed was a garden, the servant picked vast arrays of flowers, he would watch bees fly through the open window, their velvet bones rolling in yellow pollen. I remember the color...these obsessive details, how asparagus looks on his plate and the joys of heavenly perfume it creates a minute later, he does not mention fig or artichoke.

Standing back, like woman standing alone in the window, her eyes looking back on another night. From a city of changed light and heat, the Perfume River flows, the night turns, the Poet spoke: if women do not write how can they live past the time of a life time. Then music is in the river and air, winged cloud with silver dollar rain and morning was breaking when the Artist returned.

Coffee and jam on fresh morning croissant. Time and distance had not staled them; that morning she wrote of grainy mist. From somewhere in the city she wrote again. He could see everything clearly-this handful of words inhabited by friends and acquaintances (of life) she sent me. Mané treasured them like diamond cabochon. She told him to hold on to the art. Know the Artist in simple weaving, in the full ways of the ocean. There was simplicity in the message, the way she drew in the chapters of her dreams.

Non-linear is to your plot, comes from the painting world. You create images not in lines, the Artist said, but in a cluster of points – sentence fragments. But writing must be clear in a fragment. Poet, you understood my fragments, I watched you. You wrote them down in your notebook.

As for you, I would tie a greenstone fish bone around your neck, stone & desire… recalling to some original time, conjured up which cannot be measured, eyes open to moments of eventuality, to dreams and places or unreality *(single or with many folds)* as though we fell unconscious and at the edge of this world, gently pull each other ashore. Then she vanished and he woke, the sun rising above the ocean, black tui among the red flame tree. Take seeds of flame tree…take manuka flower…the leaf of kowhai…take greenstone… and hone it. Sell what you cannot carry.

He understood everything… *(of making white salt)* the sound of bird and waves on the horizon, the cold and the old, the stillness of death. And the living with an Artist, still to do… yet you tell several loosely connected stories, a central event, a loss… but the event does not follow any chain of cause and effect. The narrator reminisces about various incidents in her life- meeting an artist who later becomes her long-term lover, speaking to a ghost of a shepherd, the incidents of sex. No event takes precedence over another – although you could argue, the Artist said, that in a way the small take precedence over the all.

Did the Poet know something about the women, how they shuffled river stones in a metal pan and separated out the gold.

Or was she repeating a legend. Remembering, somewhere, the feeling of bone needle in her hand. The leather binding on wrist, twisting waxed twine and snapping it between her teeth. At the threshold, it was the same repeated pattern, of memory, of loss.

With dreaming. Fragments are separated. Just as a poem, between stanza's a pause to separate. Fragmentary form, a manner of spacing. *Il s'agit de*, the detail, thought of in a different time, yet it was the same when she compares patterns now with ancient counterpoint from a long time. Of the known and the unknown. A series of images deployed as a work of memory in a contemplative and impressionistic way. Look at a corner of the world where men paint legends on inanimate objects, on mulberry bark, hung stiff as if air-dried & starched, finger in blood, stick brushes dipped in rusty tar, liver crayon (the color of earth).

The poetic moments accumulate and form patterns and as he reads them, you get the impressions of longing and nostalgia. Eros seems to be the driving force of composition, the Artist said. While he feels his imagination stirring, accepts the woman found in his bed, as a sign of destiny, and because she holds him hostage, how many nights he will spend with her, he wonders. I make love to you so that I may take the part of a Lover. I will make unending love to you with my lips, my hands, my eyes, with all my body as long as I continue to breathe. I love making love to you. We are consumed in the very act of it.

What does desire translate to?

All desire is desirable. Whispering to me: all desire is translatable.

What marks the chapters is the actual motion your hand carries out. The right hand page folded over and smoothed into place where it becomes the left hand page, and the hand moves across the two-page surface, like an incantation of hand motions per-formed over the book - as you read the rooms of dreams and our imaginings. Do we review it later in a book. In a painting? Consider this living… as art or writing…a later composition? The second picture, painted close up, takes in the bed. It exists as a background for a woman painted. Against a double bed with white linen sheets (no blankets) the contour lines of her natural body, the curves reveal the shapes, the lines are clearer and darker in the foreground (the body of you, how I see you, how I position you and the position of light as it falls on your shoulders, like the touch of a warm cloth).

His brush moves on the canvas; cambium white air; she seems unconcerned when it begins to accumulate on her breasts and throat. She is wearing a greenstone carving on a plaited string she ties in a knot; the closures so light, it seems that a slight wind could open them, but they hold together and only her fingers can disturb them. A beautiful woman. She does not appear detached from the background, but appears to be waiting. The bed at the head and foot is deliberately ornate, an object in relief, pale gold in part, probably gilded: painted fruits & convolvulus vines, twisting upwards into a red sky heavy with crackled oils and rich tempera as if painted by the hands.

The Lovers are in the room. The door is opened; or the door opens itself. The Lovers find themselves, once again, in a situation where a poet asks us to stop and stand amazed before an act of love-making, and you may rightly protest that we have been performing equal acts of sex over the course of a thousand lines of poetry for three books. And in a hundred drawings of naked women, you have seen enough nakedness to understand the implications of flesh. Yet you are compelled to look through the door again and see what is suddenly seen.

Then you invited me into your bed. Your gossamer sarong, as wrapping around your waist, watching how you untie it, slow, interrupted by a simple hard knot.

A marriage is taking place here. On the bed is the Artist, making love to the virgin, artist's model, stranger, lover, fortuneteller, the poet: with all women in the intercourse of civilization, the tribe of women. I believe so. If you go before me, leave the door open with your shoe.

PART V

I

Dumas's charcoal works include a series of shadowy images both sensual and revealing. The dark charcoal, seamless, the balance of texture becomes a metaphor for spirituality, creating a series that reveals the feminine aspect of God in the female form.

On the surface, a system of Angels. Each protruding scapula rendered, its attached formal properties of light and shadow, encompasses the rudiments of her wings. Being aerial she is mobile and yet she stays in one place, rarely moving to another. She can show and discover things that are hidden. Fetch, carry, and do anything in the world. And discover the secrets of kings or lovers.

Why should the men have listened to the woman? Were you capable of predicting the future? Mané asked.

The power of prediction occurs in moments of belief. An inescapable fact, like a woman... as complex and delicious as baroque fantasies, masked or unmasked, filling large canvasses with puckering lips and voluptuous limbs; *Dumas treats the nude as part of a landscape that is actually a body of color and form. Deliberately romanticized images, the Artist converts you to her thoughts and passions. Portrayed as a woman of substance, not an erotized one merely posing as his Muse and his model.*

The same triptych gives a relationship between model and artist. Suggesting a real world intimacy between the Artist and his Muses. Issues of composition come to light. Dumas's woman appears on the verge of abstract, her arm bends forming a blade like image, some say a sword, as if she was a woman defending her position. Her shoulder blades protrude upwards, creating a horizon –like line. In this reactive pose, she is also the artist, with her mysteries and beliefs, revealed in gradated lines of her palm but Mané does not see this. There is a profound sense of secrecy, as if someone could see into the future, but would not reveal destiny to her unless she asks them.

Will my journey be the same as my Lover's, the pages when I look back over the pages?

There is no weight in words, and the future holds the same light, as if you are writing with water. The weather days rehearsed, the way rain stings your eyes and yet the drops are not salted. And you cannot tell where the rain starts and your tears end the moment before. A small depression holds nothing but grains of salt. Fragments of raw glass & snake-threads of flattened gold. I see him tying them on a string around your neck. What is it for?

For holding sadness.

II

The Artist loves you as if he would die tomorrow.

The Fortune Teller drew in a deep breath and traced an invisible route on a palm. Because, you know, when you sleep you are not sure to wake, and if you wake up, you are not sure to lie down again. It is like crossing any boarder, you take only what you need and leave behind the person you thought you were; you keep moving forward without looking back. There are obstacles to love and destiny. See, some cards here are decorated with broken hearts, she said. Fortune. Then I see misfortune.

You mean a fortune missed. Misplaced?

She looked closer. In the hieroglyphics of future revealed on a woman's perspiring hand, there was a house and at the foot of the tower, close to the thunder and waves, water breaking against the cliffs. It seemed like a shipwreck. It is still salvageable, if you know how to proceed without drowning. First, take note…there are men above in corporate towers with hidden agendas. Among voices accumulated was one of a woman. The bones of the dead she held in her hand directed Mané's fortune. She shook them rapidly and tipped the ivory dice on the table. The drawing offers a partial view of the woman's face in a sharply reactive dream. In each sketch, the Artist is sleeping unmindfully as the woman enters.

Watch out for a dark haired woman entering your house under the guise of a friend. She is younger than you and appears to be smiling. Do not let Mané believe what she says. They will use her to drown him. If he falls, there will be a splash that will make the world tremble. I see two people, both fallen among the birds and

79

horses, the one that received some men with sweet notes, the other bites your hand with sharp teeth. Forge or mint, stamp, and anvil, counterfeit in oblique twists on the branches. The tree blasted with blossoms, the fault in the wind not the root. It will not be his fault. He is powerless to stop it. But unfortunately, I smell it in the air, that there will be a tragedy.

You should separate your affairs out from Mané. There are lies and deceit from these people surrounding him. Loud cries and promises. It is on the dice and in the cards that he will take a massive fall... and if he does, he will take you with him.

One other thing, the Fortune Teller said, Tell him... you should listen to your woman.

III

In his latest exhibition, it was clear that he understood profoundly the nuances and tenets of Impressionism, Cubism and Expressionism. But Dumas also understood the art of calligraphy and the intrinsic power of the brush, having being trained by a Vietnamese born calligraphy master (Quan Houng), a pioneer of Black Ink Painting Movement, Quan believed that to create something new, one must have an understanding of the past even though this may not be evident in the finished works. Quan gave Dumas a familiarity with the tools of a scholar's studio. In this room, Dumas understands the relationship of the brush& ink to the rhythm of line, the significance of black, both bold and muted, and of energy, that positive and negative space brings to a painting.

The result for Mané was that he was making art that possessed beautifully balanced internal rhythms and, at times, there were dramatic and violent contrasts within the picture plane. In another drawing, her hair is the darkest element on the paper. It spills down her back while the shadow of her spine unhinges the image, which is taken up by a storm that day.

It seems, your path is destined to be my path. Nothing is written down. But when I saw you, having filled a moment with you… you read the deep lines on my face as sadness, I did not see them that way, waiting in line for nothing of lovers in the beginning, looking back to the markers indelible, clues & prints, tattoos of two. These drawings have not been exhibited as art. Each one infiltrates his private thoughts until memory keeps him hostage.

Dumas's art has a sensitive lyricism that relates to many earlier works. Ink's raw nature enables the viewer to have a different perspective of line and form from different angles and depths. Taking the essence of simple line, in spirit and form, his use of heavy calligraphic strokes, is experimental in his quest for fusion between the body, ink and paper. The bed, the chair, the room (2003), the triptych gives an abstract view of enclosed spaces. From opulent palaces, an artist loft to a canvas tent, Dumas fitfully frames the Lover's together. Issues of composition occur.

The reverse-angle of geometric red in the background that refuses to be broken. The disparity between permanence and impermanence is apparent, formal representations of a world that actually existed, now becomes abstract. By contrast, an excavation of a iconoclastic style funeral urn, waiting to be filled, reminds us of our mortality, and a deep cord ...there are things, that may still remember us, after we are gone, in ruined houses, but the scattered brick, a heap of rusty iron.

Looking around the room I want to recompose the past for you, like a room you can walk back into.... I felt you lean over the bed and felt your breath on my cheek. I could almost hear you whispering. First, I will make love to you, and then I will make you a fortune. I could hear the crinkling of paper notes in your hand.

Distant and intimate close-up, Dumas's art positions the viewer as a voyeur in the world of human relations. Images of naked bodies forces the viewer to juxtaposition sexuality and accommodate his or her body to theirs, a perspective given such close proximity, the size of Dumas's canvas... is shocking.

For his painting, investigating the confluence and divergence of opposites, Two Fish in Moon Pool (2004) the Artist uses blue non-waterproof ink. Such an ink needs to be ground with water, corrections made by wetting and re-wetting and then blotting off wet ink with paper. The finished painting, when exposed to light, over time will fade. It was his last bottle of blue China ink.

How will you remember me?

In water. Mané. I like to think of you, standing in the shower. I knew all intricacies of reef knots and half hitch, the tattoo of a two small fish on your thigh. I was looking at where the water ends, at simple things: small rain pavilion of your tanned skin as you dry off after the shower, white towel, white tile floor. Then your smile, watching me, as I was watching you – as desire expressed on a face. A crosscurrent of earlier love, a hundred fathoms deep and all the thoughts were easier closer to the water. We are water, you said.

If they ever ask me for an identifying mark, I will tell them it is just a bluish bruise. No, I will tell them: you can swim like the others; you will never forget how to swim. Later you invited me into your bath. Memory of water is inside us, reminders of forgotten things: of umbilical, semen, tears, blood – theses rivers we've never seen inside, run between within our frames. The woman you touched still here. The tribes of Veniti. The Curiovolitae skin & water seams and Asimii. Amorica sounds like gentle bite where love stings first, or waterbreaths beautiful origin for you.

Face to face, as I lay in the bed, in the first light, as I woke before you open your eyes. I would look at your face, your dark hair, skin seasoned by saltwater and time , tanned where the sun touched you… (the water smell of salt foam as if you swallowed the sea) and you wake as if I am waking myself, feel your pulse pulling inside me, like heart beads I am stringing. I can hear, within each beat rain during the night. Sometimes I wake up without you and thoughts rise like a river and flood the heart. I wonder, in those moments, what keeps me from drowning. The night still and almost warm.

I found in dreams a place of wind & wild flowers & seaweed, rock crevices full of pearly shrimps brought back from this Pacifica world where color, like love, like life, was returnable. There are degrees of existence, like degrees of heat and chill. And Lovers do not exist without the effect of heat on each other.

They bare signs of habitation of body when apart. I must have looked sad, because you spoke in a voice that was warm like summer, Mané said.

The diptych on his easel, (no date given) denotes the passage of summer with the painting on linen depicting a perfect moment. Yet, while the 23-carat gold-leafed panel in the center signifies preservation, it is tarnished by what the artist believes to be fabricated imperfections. We need time, he said, to alter life to a degree.

IV

I see the dreamers, how things appeared to be in a moment, behind and beyond it when you let go your grip on the past: The sun always shining yellow neon after the rain. I want to read the book of dreaming and forgetting. Of transparency of fish slipping in fresh blue waves. Waves breaking backwards, and fishing canoes coming home. Some beautifully assembled thoughts I discovered. Some secret seduction in the waters of the ocean, when you carried me from the ocean to the sand, where you dried me with your body.

By now, I see handwriting in mauve folio of sandpages entered after a north west storm. It is easy, sitting here in the sand at low tide, deciphering chips of missing rocks & broken stones, curved comb interweaving sea kelp's damp darkened hair. Unraveled in the riddle of king tides, crippled blue stingers littering lip of shore. Serpentine jelly ribbons, long flowing like a poisonous river, crisscrossing the sand.

When we kiss, I taste salt that had been carried on our skin, like pollen from infinite oceans, the ways of the sea and us. A frieze of seascape by a law of nature I remember you Lover, opening the basket, a long time ago and when I looked inside, the translucence of tua-tua are white glitter & water-silk iridescence of paua shells gathered up in a flax basket. We fill a bucket with seawater and you put them in deep soak. They are still alive. And they spit sand overnight. Then we simmer them in a cast iron pot. Dip them in vinegar .That's all we need to do. Our needs are simple. There were many days when we gather shellfish at the rocky inlet near the headland. Some shellfish forbidden, the green-tipped mussels we smuggled. We stayed in the foam, only long enough to steal them. It was strange, two people walking along the beachfront, talking as we walked, holding a flax basket between us The people turning around, staring at the bulging basket dripping with fat shells inside... looking back at us with growing recognition.

What did they know?

At first, this was difficult for me, being taught not to break ceremony & rules & flaws in half-truths in the whitewash of household things they told me a long time before. That is all I knew of it. These city bindings. But then you taught me how to unravel normal, shake rules from my blood. You showed me the old world, nomad, gypsy, a raider, a sailor, to live without apologies, how to be a woman at the place of rocks, this felt primitive and real. How the beach was survival, gave us food and warm sun that did not wear out. A place we found that shines and burnishes us, and unlike the city, does not tarnish us. That was how the days went.

Dumas's imagery often deals with issues. In the luck & destiny of red scarlet fish (2003) are set free. Swimming down into the water. If there is any luck to them.

We loosen the mouth of the net. We each caught similar fish. Seeing you smiling holding fish against a backdrop of blue pacific ocean, that photograph of us kissing, I found in an old picture frame, a pencil drawing you made for me Mané, of me sleeping in the sun. Straw mat. The sun thinning lines of trees as cast sundial shadow over my eyes... in the background, a section of faded driftwood fence, the remainder stretching from dunes to the foreshore, posts and rusted wire tangled by a sacred hand.

Above, a thin blue strand of dragonflies. They see us. They navigate coming closer to watch us. We are signposts. Their cellophane wings beating in a line above the rocks. We waved. But insects with tiny wings have no hands. Then the west coast sunset, as it is, red, crimson pohutukawa pregnant with blossom. Ruling the evening, an enormous ruby sun setting in hypnotic ocean and the flat sea was green verdigris.

V

I follow every set of footprints, thinking the big toe indents were his, only to discover them disappearing and reappearing. Sometimes into the surf. I continued to follow footprints until I made out a familiar shape, sitting in the same place were we had sat that first morning. The Artist watched me approach, with a smile on his face, a carbon pencil in one hand, closer up, I could see that he had drawn me in a series of kinetic shapes, as if each step I made was interpreted as staccato or outline then a simple curving and always with a thin dog drawn... following my heels. He finished the drawing, writing the date in the corner in a definitive action that gave a sense of time and reality to a moment. But there is no dog, I said. That was you, chasing your tail to find me, he said.

Do you get self-conscious when I stare at you?

How can you tell?

From your face. I can see it.

You have such a different way of looking. Sometimes it unnerves me. This artistic way of seeing, since artists, they have over centuries a distinct vision destined to reproduce creative thought, I don't know how to explain. But your eyes look deeper into what you desire and take possession of it. That look of seeing. As if you see more of me and in this consciousness: I appear. And yet, you take me by surprise.

I see you, I know you and I want you, the Artist said. Your image generates other images. Each line is physical. If I look at you, - perhaps now, how your hair falls over your shoulder and the sun catches and spins strands into gold- or the way the wind blows your hair away from your eyes- even ten seconds later...the image will hold itself. If I imagine you on the beach many years from now, you will not become lost to me: it will be like this moment, as if dreams continue where we left them the night before. Immersed in these memories, I continued to draw a nude woman curved and white, her lips like an eclipse of a dreamer's eye, was starting its smile. I was overcome with this returning.

You were master of love, Mané said, a woman's mouth as Mona Lisa. Your body was sacred, so carnal they made us love each other a hundred thousand times and the woman remembered me.

It should be as simple as footprints. Somewhere between waking and sleeping, I think of these moments, returning across days, to the way I knew blue felt in mornings, as water, then earth and sun stirs past us, like a bed of embers, an unending ribbon of heat. The waves of phosphorescence and lucid lines of sand for lovers to find in the morning. I should follow your wet footprints the prints of each step, each time your foot moved. A door opened. In it, in the room, he saw her, in her towel, her hair tied back behind her head. She closed the door, reached up and put her arms around his neck.

First, there was the scent of her, of salt water and newly washed skin. Then, across her face... a flash of emotion like lightening .This face was transfigured with love for him; her wet lips, her eyes appeared to be lit by some inner light, flames warming her flesh. Her blood, her nerves radiating heat, intense and penetrating. I have come to know the image as I draw your face, one expression familiar, found like a look in the distance, and yet in some form or contradiction a woman I do not remember her as a god and not god, stone and not stone, that hardness snapping off, that sound, to see her walking alone, in the cold rain, under the screeching sea gulls, surrounded by the wing-beats of silver fish flying back into the waves.

VI

Earlier themes continue as he explores the structures of the human body and organic shapes that makes each work open to wide interpretation. Knowing something of the dramas and struggles of his life one might suggest, that the differences came about through life changing events. Lightness and darkness, tension and softness, tumultuous explosions of emotion and thoughtfully brushed lines and a sense of love about the woman and an engaging revelation of self are all present in Dumas's body of work. Here, explicitness is softened by varying the lines, altering the angle of the charcoal as tone builds up, made lighter and darker as pressure is applied, then blended with a finger or soft eraser.

An *Island Most Fertile (2003)*. I could taste is on my lips. The grapes sweet skinned, thick and juicy. I could hear the rich harvest growing out of season. I thought I was seeing some delicious swelling and curving, the genesis of all our beginnings in the beautiful juice and pulp. Later she brings in a plate of black grapes from the kitchen.
In the dead of winter and the beginning of January, how did you come by these grapes? Mané asked.

Imagine the year is divided into two circles over the whole world, that when there is winter with us, in the opposite circle it is summer in them, as in India and countries in the east, there is always a place of sun and grapes and wine.

For exhibition: as a way to explore the mixture of distance and intimacy in close-up relationships, Mané's art places the viewer in the honey-lit room. House and Universe (no date given), desire and exhaustion that we associate with a word: bedroom. When the peaks of our sky come together, Mané said, my room will have a roof: *Quand les cimes de notre ciel se rejoindrant. Ma maison aura un toit.*

In the lineage of human habitation, physically perfect Lovers live in the palaces of each other, map within a map, tent within a tent; like the nomads, the wanderers, pilgrims of the trackless road. Grass etches your feet. Rain drumming on the earth. And the sounds, beasts, hum of wild swarms. There are seeds cast before us, sweet incantations sprouting, no longer the unconscious traveler trampling into dust, now they carry the harvest of us. Living wild without regret. This Divine exile.

So you came back, Mané said.

I hardly moved from you.

PART VI

I

Dumas reinvents ink and brush through his interpretation of point, line and plane. In his mature paintings, Dumas's color echoes first hand emotions embodied by his brushstrokes. The phonetics of emotions of the land Green (2004) shows itself in his preference for the heavy application of green blue bush and water, the frescos of poetics, influences from two islands, nostalgic, they wrote. An artist expressing his state of solitude and displacement during that experimental time. Certain colors should always be mixed on the palette. These include Ultramarine, which has a tendency to set hard when left to a paste, and white. Colors such as Pacific Blue will last as a paste. Two different blues, Mané said, may be applied with the same stroke.

No painting can exist without the tension of what it is composed of... and what it is physically made of. Dumas's use of color in Saltwater (2004) preserves the glyphs of blue Pacific Ocean with patterns of yellow sunlight piercing God-like through white clouds. The second hand image borrowed from memory, explains, the Artist said, why the blue ink refuses to dry.

Before the city, before buildings were arranged – we stayed closer to the sea. Once we were all saltwater, the legend traced back by the whale, from the days when blue-skinned mammals slowed the ships as the drift for the glassy passage to the islands. These islands of Aoteoroa, covered in a long primal cloud, cutting a pause in the sacred bush. Between these two islands...as if thoughts are inlay, or overlay ... there are deep channels cut by a sacred hand, a handclasp dissolving and reforming, the great hand dividing land that joined Aotearoa together.

Somewhere the dirt, rivers, and sky joined hands in a time that was not so ordinary. So the women came. By canoe. By steam ship. To land of motion & memories, faded as an ancient tapestry on a vast wall, by man, not by the sun. Embroidered: I have no refuge in the world. Other than my threshold. My head has no protection other than this archway. The work of a Woman in this sacred place.

Fabric & flowers, uncovering wild fruit, trailing clothes in the grass, nature is the raw material from which memory is shaped, delicate butterfly & birds in haze. Weft and weave, tendrils & trailing leaves. How the colors changed in the field. Crewel wool embroideries, silver nutmegs and pears. Until a stranger who found me sleeping in a room laden with birds of paradise in the fabric: Pacifica of lime geckos fighting on the ledge of ginger leaf, bush of kowhai and kaka tree, green moss & fern. Native bush of wet dark velvet outside the door, with the odor of green resin. And Kowhai trees pregnant with yellow pollen, soft and cocooned. When I leave the window open, the sound further into the room, of surf pulled towards us... puckering up over sand, then thrown back as deep sound-boom. I dream in yellow and green.

The bride vessel passes and veiling of eyes bleared and blind to differences, believing unevenness was even. Into angles and crevices, between fullness and emptiness looking over the railings , not to the lights of the city but to the flickering of fires burning tea-tree and manuka that some wrote gave off the same odor of honey & green resin of northern forests: in the beginning it was our own legend: then time slips forward a notch.

Your river runs through my veins. Your wild birds still follow the canoe. We never left each other, Mané. That is the truth as I know it. Sounds of us came back to us first. I turned and looked at him. I was holding out my wrists to him as if tied with imaginary rope. Untie me, Lover, I whisper.

First, tell me everything you remember of us, the Artist said, as if believing I was cross-examining destiny & fate and the workings of the universe.

Lulled by the sound of waves... A hot evening with a tingle of exposé. She turns her head, her face, and her mouth. Pay particular attention to the taste. Each faint trace of passion fruit and guava leaks on his tongue. Now you are closest to the essence. Along the edge, the ghosts are gathering. These are the emissaries of remembered things as I bruise your lips with my teeth. Some weight you feel, as a guava stone in your mouth feels like a rock on your tongue, because the pressure is not something you can see.

II

We returned many other summers with the rituals of shaking out the bedding and ceremonies of cracking open scallop shells with a diver's knife. As years passed, the children left the tin bucket and spade in the sand, falling in love until they returned just for an afternoon, and the secret trail down to the beach became overgrown with indestructible wild ginger, rusted wallflowers and orange flowering nasturtiums. Overhead the sudden burst of scarlet blossoms falling from the Christ tree like a cloak of fresh blood .The trees caught my eye like fire on the hill.

The sun is hot and yellow. It scorches ribbons of clouds and the blue sky. It's the ghostly shriek of tui; dies and comes back to life; every native bird carries in him the memory of bush that is always damp, the vague stirring of leaves, and the immense brown hand that covers the earth. We are left alone with the leaves, with all the leaves, fanned out, turn rotten then silver filigree skeletons, they give you a feeling of bare feet where ghosts come and go. Bones, spears, shells, bone hooks, woven baskets with purple kumera. Down to earth, the root and seed in detritus of hummus, back up to leaves, how many days did the rain spill over them.

Kick off these shoes. Walking down, the Artist and a barefoot Poet, follow the path through its rocks and shells, went down to the track to the remote bay with its white horseshoe and blue ocean. On the way down, before the last rock step, there was a sign warning about drowning, painted on white washed planks. A strong opaque white. How many have read? How many have read the warning? How many eyes on the white plank? The serif, comma, and question mark. How many eyes have worn away the letters, onto the rock, making the ink run down, darkening and staining the crowd of rocks on the headland? You were overwhelmed by the gusts of ocean, the strong salted brine and sharp iodine, wet kelp necklace; kiss the woman, the smell from the sea still fresh on her, the heady jasmine mingled with amber resin of kauri gum.

Nothing changes the fabric of dreams and in (here in a dream) depth of webs and patterns of compacted feather lightness woven into cloaks, plaiting baskets for sifting crayfish but some felt cold lead musket rain. Other women accepted heavy wool blankets, mothy and warm. The legends die. But then, the bones blossom. The voices return: Part saint, part warrior, part nurse, part creator, part lover.

The women speak, talking as they do - around the wooden tables in the street, repeating moments manufactured from genetics & memories. Living the way they did in old time. I hear them as if I know them well, as I know the loneliest part of the beach, the remote cove, between thick columns of pohutukawa trees anchored in wounded cliffs that are red and yellow with clay, but the roots dig in, through its history because warrior blood runs red in the taproots, they are bound with crimson blossoms, stained to the green leaves with blood, they are trees of the bush spirits ,bowing their head to the ground, one island on the map of the world and its green leaves give coolness and shade by the Pacific Ocean.

Across the blue air, the black iron sand sees something moving over there, The women with babies in their bellies. Beside the river, they swell and enter. Know years that are so far away, reconstruct them, the thick heat held power in the stones, our fire-pit, a deep black hole, vegetables and fish trapped in woven baskets, the scales weighted down under a blanket of wet flax, cold fish eyes drowned by air, with a flash of spear, warriors fighting together, rigor mortis silence as if all the loss of the world comes and goes from here.

The late afternoon enters the composition. Soft breezes, leftover from trade winds, etching sand across bare feet. The Artist moves the image closer to the sand; then to move a color down her throat, back, and waist; then he moves his charcoal back and forth over her thighs as she lies horizontally on the ground; then smudges her skin with an oil pastel across the image foreground , in one drawing he pulls her body closer to him. On paper, he moves her arm. In reality, she moves her arm to block the sun from her eyes.

In the painting, you see the woman and the Artist and in the distance, *Lion Rock & Volcanic Headlands*, (2004) and on the horizon, a fishing boat trawling for scallops just outside the limited fishing zone. Focus your attention on the boat, see shark-fins drying in the sun and the boat appears to be anchored, no one on deck, as if the crew is sleeping, then you see the couple.

(*Tell me*) you are right back there on the beach, (*ask them a question*) (*are you still lovers?*) On paper, the woman is silent. In reality, she answers the question: We lay side by side in the sand. Brushing one image across the surface of another image (*say what you see so we know you are feeling*) his lips on your lips, something between breaths colliding, how else to describe desire (*then imagine the lips of another man*).

When I try this, the Artist starts smiling. But when you imagine the lips of another, of others and their desire to know you and who desert you late at night and you wash your face in the sea. Midnight, your face in the moonlight, a stranger walking by, staring into her eyes, he could not tell salt water from her tears.

Others have loved you and deserted you, it is true, but the Artist's face in front of you, now appears more Adonis, sculptured and strong featured than when you imagined other men. No, I want his warm salty mouth locked in mine. No other. As though somewhere a porthole had been smashed and the sea air permitted to pour into a long sealed space (*looking directly into his eyes*), (*look closely at the color*), your eyes close; (*focus on this and how that effects you*). Focus on this moment, (*on this image), (and tell me whether)* you can feel his hands through the pareo tied around your waist, when you see him lying on the sand (*superimposed in the middle of the picture),* so I know you have gone back there with him.

III

Memory of water. The light from the sun filters through the surface a ribbon of sapphires. Not solid gems but tiny particles crushed as if they were ultramarine blue cerulean ground by a great pestle: Prussian blue to cobalt with tinctures of indigo and shades of lapis, It is like swimming into all the beach glass of civilization sparkling before us. I saw the same blue in your eyes. When we were skin diving, holding on to each other's arms, looking into your face. The water holds us like a secret.

And drawing a deep breath I turned over and let my body sink. I caught up with you in the marine cave where blue mau fish, curve up and part the seam of ocean like a curtain, and we swim through, past the dead weight of dark volcanic rock rooted on the floor. I recognize the door of the metal cage, filled with decomposing snapper heads and slime weed, the trap full of crayfish who enter the room to feast and forget how to leave. The undersized and the females carrying eggs under the tails are set free.

What is it?

I used to trap things and kill things, Mané said. As a boy. As a Man. Tap the side of a nest and grab the neck of a baby bird. Shake it like a child until I broke it, in the bush all trees were mine, kohai, kauri and pine held fantail embryos, a few tui, one bellbird, speckled garden thrush, common brown sparrow and a thousand blue blackbird eggs and then to prick with a stainless pin, lips placed as a bullet on cold hard shell, the force of a child's seven year breath blows bloody vein yolk.

Old man. Old man. Teach me to fish. Teach me to rip skin off possums. Let me keep one pelt. Gave me wax thread and curved sail needle. Alone in my room, I make a hunting hat of rust colour fur. Old Man. Old man teach me to bait a hook. Wrench a fish from the arms of the sea. Once I was the hunter... then I was hunted, the Artist said.

I know, Mané. I touched my fingers to his lips. I know because they hunted me too.

Do you believe in universal retribution for the hunter...to feel what it is like to be followed, trapped or cut down?

Some part of me does, he said.

Is what you imagine, more real that what you see? I ask.

The Artist smiles. I see origins of you, he said. Both you and the drawing brings into being things that have not existed before in the world. I have drawn you so many times and I have shown that art comes because there are techniques for reproducing the deep structure of perception. It is like solving the mystery of image making and believing that I have not yet begun to understand the interior of you or these images of you. But sometimes I see through the tissues and tracings between us, or a specific color- the blue of the ocean- will flash for a moment, it brings the sand and waves on the West Coast, it has a certain dark iron sand and deep green bush-light, they must have a word for this creative process or know that we will need one, between us and art.

It is the time of day- sun's crimson rays are falling back into blue print of horizon. We stare out at a blank of flat sea, where the waves spread out and hide tiny shells chipped by the waves, a faint scrim of early waves swelling...when the waves spell storm and hurricane and fish move closer into the net. Mané sat, arranging driftwood onto the fire. As if he is a builder, he piles the salt-bleached logs in a strong structure, leaving deliberate spaces for fire to breathe. He lights the fire, using matches he has inside his jacket. And as the fire burns of its own accord, he picks up the soft wool blanket, unfolds it and smoothes it between practiced fingers, wraps it around us both, the delicate feel of cloth against skin.

The composition on the beach: sand blows through my mind- it catches in our hair, dusts over arms and legs with emery grit. - the sand holds the print of a footstep; we take turns stepping into each others marks, *touching you with bare feet as if my soul is walking on you*, a foot reversing the location of toe and heal; sand is the material in which the print is made, like the sandal under Hermes' feet.

Yet, these movements are not rehearsed, Mané said. When I walk with you, from the far end of the beach, the filmy pareo lifted high and tucked into the lip of your underwear. One hand holding my hand. One holding a shell, (a *rare sea-blossom*). A sidestep seen from the back, but, this was no opening step. Some external force seems to know us.

The white beach seems infinite. It was only at the end of the beach I saw some people. These were naked men. In strip between the barbed wire fence that held the bush back from the sand and the ocean, There were men embracing in the water, like shiny fish. Their broad backs shimmering muscle tight rough waves, thrashing about in the shoals. I watched in the wake of abandoned fish, as the long trident of water slammed down on the water and the waves sucked them under. Then they lifted not the fishes up, but this pale corpse, neck broken and eaten by worms in the waves, heavy head dangling, the bleached fat and stringy guts and sinew exposed to salt brine, oval skull gleaming in the bright sun as the tide brought disfigurement to the sands.

It was not a man, but a broken fur seal, which had floated in with the tides before lying on the sand at my feet. It was growing late.

Suddenly the sound of the black dog barking to wake the lost seal. The wail of a strange bird up in the evening sky seemed to signal the black-back gulls to find us here. Looking down they saw the man. The man. Black dog. Dead seal. In the darkening loneliness of the Piha beach, the sight was unknown to them.

Sometimes I painted what I saw. Naked men. Dead seal. The woman said that I would fill her head with dark images. From the silence, from the gray clouding her eyes, I knew the exact spot the images entered and she asked if I could tell her where the beautiful ones were. Give me beautiful images, she said. In a few words, I told her.

We stand on the same land. The little patch of shrine where we hold each other. What is yours is mine. There is nothing to indicate that our existence has been overlooked or forgotten in this place, the circles of sun and moon render the same illusion, day after night. An aura of the other, like a halo, we are seen together in the same highly saturated tones.

I look around. Back to the rim of tea-tree bush and fingers of flaxes red flowers. Yes. This is the same land, I follow in the footsteps of others... enter the land, the caves, tents, shacks and mansions, unlock the rusty portals of every place we have ever entered or re-entered. It is scattered with refuse, arrowheads and shrines. Time lost in concrete sundial, broken wristwatch, overgrown topiary. All these things and none of these things matter. It is the offerings from the janitors, cleaners, keepers of humanity. It is the space left by pilgrims' exodus.

Hanging from driven nail thin and worn by salt, hung a plaited leather necklace with a carved greenstone pendant and under the necklace a silver cross tied on string, features of a miniature Saint. His feet and hands nailed down. His eyes looking out from under a wreath of metal thorns. It was very still when I picked it up and held it in my fingers, necklace of thorns and suffering , I felt the cold of stone, and something like a drop of blood. It was the thorns scratching my cheek. The Poet cannot be afraid, the thorns are barely painful, drops of blood in my mouth, and my feet slip on the leaves. The lesson of sacrament. Until every correlation between two people is given away and found. The ceremonies would go on. To my amazement, he opens his eyes, two dark eyes, two arrows shot magnetic into the night sky and the stars that remained looked freshly washed with rain.

If I go some distance away from you, Mané, I will be able to recognize who you are because of you, and if I go further away I will still recognize you, further away and distance will still not diminish the way I feel. For this law of distance does not apply to your body (I see the man you are) and I loved you just the same, masculine torso in oak mirror frame (confirmed by experience) what you do for me; the whole horizon enters, life's aperture of what I see may be sometimes in shadow, as is the nature of holes, that the images intermingle within the light of the night, and I see you in dark and black, as I am, when we make love a black hole that holds everything closer (to be able to say, a secret space) it is warm in here, not so much a hole but a cave. Our secret cave: where this love multiplies and reproduces (images in an annex room) all bodies falling together and all of us bearing the ropes and rudder of this life.

IV

A Man & Woman have places in their heart that do not yet exist and into them enters another in order that they may have existence. Some days I feel like such great powers had been watching me on this journey. To follow me a long way to this first world, the entrance place. Sometimes I feel her cool embrace as a benevolent ghost looking out for me. Small figure who sang the old songs.

I know ghosts. I feel them. Then I feel her, the ghost, her sad arms hugging my shoulders.

I can't forget what I dreamed last night: in a faraway Asia, a Poet and an Artist survived on mango and delicate feelings. Her eyes are now colored by fate, her beautiful green eyes shadowed by circumstance. Is it us Mané.

Half asleep, he thinks, never, she has changed and yet there is something soft about her, unchanged, and she has known stillness. And quiet, the words grow around us; the rooms and houses look familiar, the cities and countryside, the water, warm and ancient. Memories awake now, the relics of sensation returning, scars of your smile, coloring red, and that face made hard and everlasting stone, smiles as the man fixes it, and in this world, how many women has he left smiling.

We are mourners in the moment. But with the disquiet that stillness brings. There are ghosts everywhere. We were as quiet as if honoring all ghosts who pass before us. As we will pass away and others will remember our dead laugh, inside the silences. Then, this thick wet canvas. Black drawing of night. Venus. The stanza of jet and silk, its seductive lines slipping off paper, the drawing keeps up its quiet breathing, as if breathing is some law of living, carving familiar sound from air held in a room. The fragrant. The wild scent of you, the dark scent of chocolate. You understand, he said, and put his hand in mine. That is the mix-up of all loving. It is not perfect. Just human.

V

So we make love, using up our life in a slow way, among our heartbeats. These pillows and sheets, this trousseau was once her trophy before she was a woman, in parts faded and small repairs bequeathed. I turned to him. And tears came to my eyes. I understand these imperfections, the bruises of failure, I said, I feel them inside myself. And yet, I still could not stand there at the citadel of truth and tell him honestly everything I knew, to reconstruct from the faded desires, unforgotten loves which are reborn in a memory. I have a memory of you.

Before I knew, it was your eyes looking at me from the corner of a room. The mornings when everything appears to be normal and fugitive feelings burst in, dictating a secret dossier. For example: ... the long afternoons... the crumpled sheets... I should be telling you this... somewhere in black and white, there is a room. And in the room, I am there, but not alone.

This negative taken in the backroom, the hotel by the river, old memories surface now... I can see the river from the window, snow damned in an ice flow, like ages ago... and breath as rusted fog, the trees skeletons against winter sky, their icicle branches frozen together like reindeer antlers. These were two trees pollinated by wind in the ancient forest .An accidental fusion of human creativity and irrepressible natural process. It belongs to a forest, but deep forests there is a smell of ghosts. All trees were burning when I looked back.

The author of illicit affairs watching me, I caught his eye like fire on the hill: I was warm, the room a fire blazing, and the panels of oak on the walls, the bed posts were medieval, carved in wooden roses and heavy velvet curtains pushed to the side. As if one desires to draw them across .And turning back to the bed, linen sheets with a tiny thread count, template the size of a pinhead, and a quilt with crewel embroideries, delicate explosions of kisses bursting like ripe berries, the tree of clandestine life and a stitched tapestry on the wall like a faded fresco among the rainbow curve of the simplest herb embankment, of pilgrims or saints or invisible angels might merge together and say a combined prayer for the journey, with the roots of prayer appearing and disappearing, then stopping to pluck some faded herb fall into fresh straw bed and displace it or blindfolded they might herald the morning and they were looking down at this sex as it happens to be that I was naked, charged with naked affirmation, yet fully clothed in their eyes, a cloak of a forgotten lover, yes it was winter at five o'clock, I knew by the way the sun dissolved on the wall, and the long tapers by the bed cast shadows above us.

When did I come to feel guilty for this physical pleasure as a pulse camped among the heartbeats, I was powerless to stop it while I kept breathing...in the room, the shutters fastened. And later tried to hypnotize my memory, like a bicameral trophy of this illicit moment, lead-weighted with all that collects mercurial, its heavy secret could poison promises I made to you, in the old church, like echo as some sinners or a choir of unnamed boys, once I thought I heard a chorus hymn of reformation, when you laid claim to my body and later I unclaimed you, but I was mistaken. I changed the rules of love, in a moment, a moment with another, on another body. Then I pressed my body closer.

How could I have known about this passionate residue that would return when you made love to me, until I believed so many mixed up things about love and fidelity, the mirror I saw my reflection in over and over again, scar tissue like a skin I should be shedding, I was the same woman naked but with a different man. Is it the ghost of love who looks back from the mist and mirage, back from my mirror, from the secret shield of ancient moments where I am the whore in the poems, the woman he paid with a kiss for all its intactness?

This tryst was a destiny but not a conclusion, did it happen as a woman escaping from rules, rules and documentation, domestication of a concubine, bindings I find unsettling. I wonder if love should be like this. Just to see what goes wrong with my loving. I act as I feel, and I am faithful if I feel like it, sometimes I wait for another to rescue me. I am aware of it, these delicate feelings. But I have confessed and you have accepted. I am conscious of the fact. If I told you this, does it mean a little atonement?

Somewhere along the way I changed lovers as I change moments, by I slipped through, without telling you. Yet when we are together, I have the feeing of complete. With the others, I was attached but not welded on to a framework, intricate, intimate, solid… as if love knows the construction or destruction, fastening, unhooking and soldering of such moments. Returning to the starting point with you. But the moment of leaving creates a new departure point. Sometimes my eyes are wet. Thoughts frozen like a river, I hold from you.

Sometimes I think you read my mind, Mané said: If you carried a cup, you would be afraid of spilling it. And because of the fact that you were afraid, you would not notice the beauty of the cup, the fragrance, the warmth of the tea- you would be too afraid of spilling, you would not notice. It is natural to get things wrong. When you said just then: Everyone makes mistakes. I knew, you were saying 'me'- I was making mistakes, but you still loved me. As if he shouted it out, as if he told me and then he agreed, it should be printed into the chapters.

I am fascinated by the way woman writes in a straight line. If every word is planted like a seed, you will find them. Printed on royal stock, the pages still look fresh. Longer than the sheets of the third folio, which is longer than the first and second folio. Printed on demy paper, the volume so large, the letterpress is shared in seven shops of female printers.

So, it is written: that when the Red River flooded, rice farmers saw the water surface as a stage. They carved puppets from water-resistant fig-tree timber and modeled the faces and bodies of men they knew. The puppets danced on ponds, lakes and flooded rice fields. Seven woman puppeteers stand in water behind a bamboo screen. In the dark, they appear to make men walk on water.

PART VII

I

Each one of us, then, should speak of his road, his crossroads, his roadside benches; each one of us should make a surveyor's map of his lost fields and meadows. Gaston Bachelard said when she showed him the articles of exposure. The ruin of the lovers where destitution is stamped with a library stamp from the observatory, then partially covered by a morocco label of a man who watched constellations. It makes a book, the Poet said. There was no time to hide imperfections that fell into the final eighteen lines of text. Creased and so printed without loss. With a closed tear in the lower margin. Your eye caught them all. Trimmed to fore-edge rules, some scattered with minor stains between strata. Earth and river poem.

Edition Two is one of the most elaborate of early treatises on secret writing, A way of sending messages without symbols of a messenger. I think it is true to say of the hotel. You stayed together and circumnavigated each other. It had a language inside the walls. A story and I was in it. So were you. No time for lovemaking, no time for talk.

So you reserved a room at the hotel and the Concierge bought up ten file boxes filled with papers and two suitcases. Looks like this isn't a relaxing weekend you have planned, he said. He waited for a tip. Your pockets were full of pens and coins. You gave him a handful of loose change and locked the door. There was no soap in the shower.

All your life was planned to now, all the city buildings familiar, pointing upwards, the glass & steel, the influence of the powerful and mighty. I asked him questions and then I said, the definition of security according to Aristotle is the absence of awareness of danger. What assurance, what dark power watches as you pass through days. It was as if you enact an old film noir black and fated. Dangerous. As if the Artist wants to feel overpowered, so he can be poor, live the ten flights of stairs to the attic garret, play the role of an Artist. I stopped suddenly, words which create high tension. I caught Mané staring into a file-box, he was bound up with the desperate and distressed, with people trapped like prisoners, of strange circumstance the rest of the world has no sympathy for. Still , it is, they said, brought on by yourself, that secretly, most artists' are involved in some intrigue, love, wanting to be discovered, wanting a drama.

The next days were overfilled. Monday, you met the lawyer at his office in the newly refurbished brothel. His foyer had photographs of famous people he had met and he displayed their signed, framed photographs, the visual acoustics for beautiful & rich, prosaic and artificial.

The caffeine-charged lawyer explained how he handled such cases. He explained his dynamic attack, his immediacy and parody of Chinese warrior philosophy , the rules of war, detailing the present conflict, like historic wars, could be solved by cunning.

I could not look at his eyes too closely. Yet I never reacted to my instincts, it was self-protection, I rationalized, he knows what he is doing, he has a reputation of exploiting others. No. Idealizing his position of authority, in which intelligence is natural. One has to trust a learned man. Not only God, but the system, morality affords its own protection, it shields us from avarices, the man acts according to the dollars you pay, his hourly charge for expertise. And he promises you and flatters himself, expect victory by his pen.

He drew Mané's attention to statements and complications, but every talk was full of influence, until you took mental notes, enough to believe and by the time he showed you to the foyer, the white marbled tiles, clinical on the floors and a fountain with fat goldfish swimming, by the steel of elevator door, the red light flashing as one fell to the ground, by the time the fish came up for air, you could not hear the threat of death by psychological murder, it seemed part of the walls.

Elaborate treatises on secret writing. All day I heard them talking in the office. Of exploiting humans at a deeper level, archaeology of the soul. Woke up to a realization. You are talking to people who are not human beings. They are materialists. If they do not believe in art. They will not believe the Artist.

I did not return to the office; I would give up self-forgetting behaviors. The room at the hotel was littered with private papers, evidential, incidental, as wide as the king bed, the morning alarm returns again; a pistol shot at the beginning of a race. Breakfast served in the room. Black coffee. White toast under a starched white napkin. Wiped butter with the wrong knife. It gave a taste of berry jam and fried bacon. It gave a taste of confusion.

Everything reaches its balance One phone call later that morning. The mistakes the lawyer made, lay like rot in the trash to feed the rats. The contracts eaten by mice; inscriptions of failures, rotting away in the law mausoleum. Mané has lost everything.

Turn out the lights and let your ghost tell the story, until we terrify ourselves. She has not yet spoken. She was a prisoner of her need to talk, until someone asked you about this period of her life, where it had taken place, believing that a woman should know how to change her destiny.

II

There is a black book in the country where you once lived. It was a winter when birds die and fishes lay stiffened fur in translucent ice, which makes even the mud and slime of warm lakes cold, a corporate heart set hard as concrete. Cold as stone. Crawling underneath, a snake twisted by knaves. Washed the viper with so much venom, force heart and nerve and sinew, there is no cure, we all die. Dogs defile your walls and wasps and hornets breed beneath your roof, for this office of falsehood, and this cave of lies. Those men, who wear a mask to hide behind, the *Legal Rodents (2002)* (a pest to humanity) the *Judgmental Assassination (*2002) it voids its own excrement and whomever it touches burns like fire and (the smell of urine often kills the weasel itself) are the ruin of humanity, you said as you cursed them all.

What was the truth. Truth was not the blackened judgment heart, shared in deeds, of others your pen an instrument of intent, to sign bitter ink with evil men. Not your own, this icy hardness a weighted danger. Legal card shufflers; they don't look too good or talk too wise. Standing higher up they deal in lies, risk dollars on a single game and never breathe a word of loss or take the blame. *Miserables Elysium & Saint Paulo (*2003). Two imposters just the same. Inside downtown offices, *Corporate Sociopathetique (2001)*, a game of inhumanity forever played ,the pieces chosen selectively, no recent deaths or bad luck., until you cross them. Although the pieces and moves are different, the objective remains the same: to steal your home. Aotearoa. I took your flag inside and burned its stars.

The closed crime and an act of stealing, they did so quietly, no other women knew how you loose the front door key, enter the

110

silence to find nothing left and the light goes off - a telephone ringing in a vacant house. Then in the empty room, only the wind's home. It has no glazing and the shutter swings, old places cannot wound you, only the memory stings. In a clap of thunder. Taken as lightening, and a vague feeling between you, that fate discharged as a shock meant for somebody else.

Every loss is wrapped in emptiness. The light you see it in. An overgrown courtyard, the leaves you used to sweep. Everything feels incomplete and who is standing out on the street. No password to release you from this place. And yet you expect bread and you have got a stone; break your teeth on it.

If perhaps, you had listened to the Fortune Teller, taken her words as truth… now homeless, shelter gone, what comes of this? Your house stands empty. People you knew walk past. They see mail crushed in the letterbox, autumn leaves piled up in the doorway. Cobwebbed keyhole, a lock that no one opens. Your palaces are stolen, bricks and words met in collision and argument and in the end both were both tricked by a legal word, victims of their practical joke, in a letter torn open by the storm, and you are locked outside, leaving the house masterless and flagless. Rooms you lived inside we now live outside of.

Remember this home for me, black metal pan with warm shrimp paella, green figs and blue china bowl the same color as the sea, and freesias yellow as summer sun. Further past the breakers. Then the ocean watching, dead verdigris harbor. And the black-back gull, dark feathers lacquered, waiting for warm sour dough bread, our returning. Then the gull cried, his orange tongue salted and parched by the brine.

Where have you gone?

Where can you go to?

You have nowhere but I am asking you to stay with me, Mané said. That the only way back home is to slip inside the seam old dreams. Now you are separated by an outline on legal paper. A few lines, signed which brought about this metamorphosis. Every room held vibrations of you, the way you superimpose one pattern on another.

By midnight, you will still be dreaming that you are at the door of the house. In your house. In your bedroom. Empty, this space in your life. There it is. You flung the emptiness out of your arms and into the open street. You had a pile of books under the bed, a red candle half burned. Every moment was cross - referenced back to you like names and kisses. I had you and we had each other in the faded fresco of the room. Until the room begins to echo, then whispers fall silent. I would let you trespass so completely our room is a familiar liar, as familiar to you as it was before I left, Mané said.

The critics wrote that Dumas's art during this period, was a reaction to unusual suffering. When one compares his life, to the suffering of European Artists, it appears Dumas knew greater misery and poverty in later years. Yet Dumas did not show bitterness. For he was not to be ground out of existence so easily. He was in a powerful place, his rupture in life becomes transmuted into works of art, contributing to his compassion for humanity. He understands other human beings may be victims, he holds society responsible and art becomes an act of vengeance.

Yet there appears an absence of emotion. Paint on canvasses. Blacking out images. An individual isolation and retraction, as if some softness in his soul perished. Looking at the Artist sleeping, looking at the hand, then the fingers, down to the moons of his fingertips, the ink shadows remain, even in sleep.

III

I feel us there, Mané. In the paper shadows, I thought that I saw you projected on a whitewashed wall. Was it, possible, I asked myself, possible to be alive and haunt a place and when I enter the rooms in my mind, someone sees me? Place it in my mind, a woman, a man, a room. Each is an image. Each is lighter than ghost to some degree. How quickly the amorphous isolation. At first, entering the room, to stand before the open window, a Man, in the past, only crossing closer than this, the woman turning to him, almost forgotten as if left in an orphanage. Later she finds her head on his shoulder. (No) The remains of human contact. Do I have to think of her to keep her alive? No end to her seasons. In the smell of grapes on the autumn table. And the moth circling the warm candle. For light? Or heat?

A woman's rhythm within him, shift of pain that is painless and motionless. What she chooses to remember. Or forget. Then have him lift her head and watch as he slowly kisses her on a mouth, to resuscitate a part of him, part her lips slightly, her lips moist.

Some proof that summer stays. The mimesis of love in the room, even though, the woman entered the room expecting to find nothing. Yes, the room is empty and we are standing there, broken and fragile. So I put my mouth against the wall and kissed it. The mouths prayer to Loss of Stones. Only warm as December. Its Gods. The wailing wall at the lands edge. A trampled wreath of wreckage. Barely prayable. Prayer for two. I become my panic. I become my fear. The thought of the house keeps me haunted- drags me down the road shaking and crying- an unfamiliar street now.

Here she closed her eyes as if she was sleeping, but her hands tightened in a fist. And then she burst out "I pass the house and watch for the thieves." There is no one home. You were passing through the street like a ghost, come to visit. You came here only a few times, but when you went away, the house occupies a place deep inside you.

The rooms are there still. And yet? Nothing new but white wisteria in Spring. Each heady bloom. The wall is in the front of the house and tangled vines covered in white. You hold them in your hand. What fragrant blossoms. You are scared of them. How sad a woman feels, standing on the street outside her home. Life giving life and tears and overwhelming losses. You wonder if life should be like this. I mean, I was often asked how you kept on living. You'll try to remember when you could barely speak. Overcome by a deep anxiety you have not experienced before, a kind of deep anguish and sadness, you wrote them all on a piece of paper. That is how I remember.

Many read nothing but our memory. Let the street be filled with the litter of legal lies masked by friendly sentiments. Sold out by the proceeds of futile action. I had no desire to see my name in print. We wait in the room with nothing to do but the words we can talk which nobody wants to hear spoken. They are less useful than dung. I am tired of the dictionary of hurt. Your tears are my tears now. And when our eyes run dry, our tears turn to crystal stars. Infinite galaxy, you show me through a telescope, star-strewn magnifications. Every thing you show me, leads me away to a point of intimacy. And you tell me it does not matter, when we are sleeping together in a tent in our thousand star hotel, so I understand the heavens from the standpoint of someone capturing life after loss.

IV

So life marooned you. It seemed you were still attached. That one lover holds another's pattern and the creases and lines pass, barely noticed. You watch the hermit crabs, stand in tide pools on the west coast beach, where there is nothing to impede your movement, you are close to green weed, kelp raisin harvest, closer to the seas current than any time in your life. It tosses up your buried past, the broken oar. And floats this empty suitcase belonging to foreign exiles, unnamed your belongings, unbelongings, tossed untidy, floating towards you, as it was in the beginning, is now in an ending. Listen.

The past has many voices; the wine in a mouth, ice is on the vine, the season grown up. Then gone the different voices echo together. Breaks of voice, breaks of glass. Each sequence as one long breath. The distant note heard in shivering. Winterfreeze moment all the voices under the silent fog, are counted, measure months lying awake, anxious calculating the future, trying to unweave, unravel and piece together the past, picking shards from glass from my mind, drops of water from a river and untangling knots from your hair, as if my fingers were a comb disowning the past and the future.

The woman fights this loss of gravity in waking dreams, she spoke to me, her nights spooled back to beginning, but not her beginning, the silent thawing of crocus flowers, melting their orange stamens taken to themselves, the emotionless reindeer orchid, tiny buried consequence of living among the dirt and freeze, so the prayer was said of the bulb in the earth, the unprayable. Prayer at the saffron annunciation. The past has no end, the buried deception of what was believed in the broken hours, future futureless, even in the attached devotion, which might pass for devotionless, on this room with a winter light, the lovers listening to the undeniable, there is a chance love stops before you wake, dirt in your mouths makes the world taste dry, and love was never ending: that is and was. Spit The dirt. It chokes you.

Let me touch you. See if my hands pass through you, Mané. Where is the end, the Artist drawing an unbreakable line. Attach me, where it holds me; bind the rope tighter around each wrist. I cannot think of a time when I need to be held more. Or think what this solidarity is, of you and me.

Evoked by this sudden illumination, you shouted. You forget the agony of others. Are we nothing special? An idealistic revolution, an evolution from your ghost? She will be returned to you one day. White linen. White paper holds its cargo of bitter ink and white feather becomes her wing. Like her ghost will pass in front of you. The backward look over a shoulder as she left. The swell of clavicle buds, concealed wires sown into restless bone, is what it always was.

Each crying ghost stays in wall & beam & rafters of my hate & pain. Denies her leaving. Cast like a sad shadow of her past. For they think all they inherit is the floors & windows and doorways. But (No) heavy sadness is papering the walls, all my grief is a frieze soon felt by you. And in the mirror by the front door, who reflects our sadness and our terrors inter fog .Mercurial slivers as thoughts seeping in my blood, as my transfusion, this rusted poison of our anguish flows further than we know. Our lives. Our tears as water poured on the ground. Faith and hope have vanished, contaminated by all men. And even love, like our blanket, grows thin.

Whose hands hold a brush and brush my hips with his hands. Those who have to do with lapis blue, cambium red, magenta. Lips. Angelus of flesh. This ink. I think it is a question. Never repeated... are we permanent? We enter the realm of touch, the lips, and

116

the deep with each other and for a moment, forget this room, the spill of light, the discontinuity of voices. Like the past, we have no destination.

But then, I go back to the same room as ghosts, he said, the silhouette of the palm tree and lantern of moonlight. I feel the vertigo too; the immense drop out of the warm bed inside this scant room, a room is not our home, a mattress low on the ground. Sheets still feel hot from our bodies as if they have been kept warm in the belly of the house. Maybe they keep pilgrims here. In the aftermath of corruption, this concrete floor consecrates our bones, the intimacy of us, nocturnal shifting moving bare under the covers. Still, I am comforted by the overlay of you, some identity of our younger selves, like faded blankets, Mané said.

V

You sound bitter, the Fortune Teller said. I tried to warn you. I saw it in the cards. I overheard corporal whispers. Mané would have lies and deceit surrounding him, of corporate manipulation by men, to separate yourself out from him... he was going to take a huge fall and he would take you with him. I warned you back then. Why did you not listen? You only listen to what you know. I could not understand this. It was as if you spoke a different language... or I was the foreigner. Have you been back to there?

I have a vague memory of vigils along the edge of the road watching our house from a distance by the bridge or under the portico of an antique store, on the off-chance that the front door would open, but like a ruined weather house, neither woman or man were inside.

Then you believe the villa is still cursed?

The Fortune Teller said: It was like a light of blackness turned against you, bad luck looked at you another way. Fortune looks at you another. So now, the woman and man by entering your home adopt this same pattern of fate and so I predict that pain and upheaval will share their human cobweb. Fate is familiar and falls easily into place and into all occupants. Soon all they loved will separate from them. As loss happened to you, and the people who lived there before you, the builder of sailboats, the two fighting spinsters, the widowed postmaster and his crippled son, the dying printmaker. And bad times are being concentrated on this house through centuries- like a burning through glass. History articulates the days before we live them.

Then two strangers moved in to our house, where great pains, upheaval and symbolic death have taken place. They could not expect to buy a house free from such a death. There is an aftermath, a time when you look back at what you are left with. I can't pull back the years torn like rags from my mind. When I stitch them up, the cost does not make sense.

I wonder, is loss temporary or is emptiness between words inside time, beyond this place? I asked. This is what you need to ask him, she said. And you can't figure the survival factor in all this. You can't dream of a future, You can't imagine. starting over, where does starting over… start? What stones do you need to rebuild a home and how many. What remembered pattern do you place them in. Rows, herringbone, like an ancient road?

The Fortune Teller said, I have no answers to give you.

VI

If I speak of our road, Lover, I shall speak of a time after loss, when you are left to count what remains on a few fingers, the lines on the palm of your hands, the fragments of a life that was, patterns, rhythms, riddles and rhymes of us in our time. I will give the past to you, in the hope that it will fade from exposure. Like a film spool pulled out before the negatives are developed, the rich pigments of hurt will be blurred and forgotten. By giving away past memories, the burden of the past will fall away from us, the Lover said. But still this sharp apex of pain, marks the extremes of life's fractured plan.

Of all that is speech there is no word of you, Of all that is heard there is a time when all love ends. We are bones, words that fall like the rain on each of us. Do we divide part of love from us? In the cool day, the tree split, in my wrist the bone was dry. For I will not honor the virgin, hold the spear, fall to hurt. the string of my eye. The dry dune, fruit of the womb, the fake cross on the hill, the still lake, and rooms we sleep in. White in the gown of bone, life still in us. As I am. Sing to the wind, and the bone sand, torn and whole, the cave near the door. I do not hope more than you gave me.

Let the word say. The land lay on us. The wing broke and will not fly. But will fan the air in vain. Air is dry, and for us rose the end to no end. In this land we own no one. At the first light, the turn of a face, the time I see a shape in the vapor of air. The bones fall and shake and wake us; the bone dry, white, fell out like stone. A ghost of river mouth.

The age of the shark, the skin of snake rolls at your feet. The fig fruit cast on a rock like a dial of a day that will pass for one more day. A slot in time. The sad scene, flute song, stops and starts, like hope in the steps of our mind, stops and starts, mouth blown, like a fly in a web, on the stair the light will fade, the steps will stop. Fade. Fade.

Crack the bone open, the chalk and rice, white grain, falls like rain. But speak the word. Walk where I walk. Speak what I dare to say. All of us sow haphazard seeds of fate .Talk to the prisoner or walk with Kings, the blessing of a crowd, blow from a foe or loving friend can hurt you in the end, insensible quota, this last lathe of wooden storm, mulch of human suffering to watch things that you gave your life to... broken. The cask bones lighted in an unforgiving minute, wick exploding, dynamite powdered dry bones.

Do not walk on the bone path. Stones cut your feet. The straw shoe will keep the rain out. Gone in white. In blue. The hue I gave you in kiss. Talk ether of silence. Who will move me when you go? Who will find your bone. As we walk the hills are far, the land is past. We will not go back. The empty walls as I had left them. A few cracked pots and glass and a fire, the ceiling filled with figures made from the smoke from a candle.

Hold my hand. Kiss me one time. Who made the bone fall like rain on the path. Who made the wine, the water, the sand, the touch of your hand. Made the stone cool, the bread warm, the sea foam, this time we own.

To traces of nothing. There is nothing that man fears more than the touch of the unknown. The bold assertion coming in at an unexpected angle. Actual loss is accidental, the Prophet said. Your places were not lost accidentally. This is done by some action. Only through some violent cause of corruption of spiritual and heaven-ly substances you cannot-be, he said.

Like a prayer a hymn a charter for the rich, for the poor , we are all cloaked in this life. You saw it coming. When we approve of the look without knowing the evil in it. His hostility is jealousy .That dark stink of him. See an advocate in his robe: think he has some ability. I have seen false attitudes, impotent lawyers become destructive

Mystery duped the world, which cannot resist the way he looks. I watched this happen: when the woman & man you trusted, forgot the exact spot that defined your life from their life. The legal tyrant, his destructiveness a sign of impotency. He forgot you. But Everyman is you, he said, the fated thread holding each of us. Close your fingers. Feel it sting your palm. Close the door in your face. All left you homeless. When a man looses so much, he wishes to sink like a stone. He forgets how to trust. Then earth swallows him. If her Artist disappears, earth will swallow the woman.

VII

Who will recognize us... years longer into this exile.

Until that moment of irrevocable loss, suffering was intermittent an interruption of disease (there will be coughing to the point of choking) or disruption by death, not perpetual suffering, as it impasses all tomorrows.

Now, future is faded ink, torn line bloody stain. Of tamed anger for things you regret. Having pressed beautiful things between pages of a book before they burned it. And the way you hope for a wrist-ful of blood, horizontal lines as some detour or distraction for the primitive terror of being alone. Or maybe as a way of using up pain by opening my veins, like the leaves of a diary, because that has never been opened. The way the knife goes is the way down, is the way down is the way back?

Let me hold your wrists in my hands, the blood and skin. I am no healer. That scars are no longer there. It is a monument. A prayer Albrecht Durer carved. Where timber ends, the fingers of vine, trailing orchid, the scented ones, perfume on a wrist. And those who took your pulse felt. Alive. The inky blue stream. Those who knew you. Their eyes wait more years for your words to reach them. The journals with silk cover, the diary plaited moleskin, not escaping form the past, your chains broke try escaping a past into different lives. You are not the same person bound to me, hand in my hand. You've changed. I've changed. And lying on this bed, watching the silken light fall gold over your face, too beautiful... you cannot think the future is finished

There is time in every moment. Shall we take what remains of us. You whose body I touch will never be repeated, by the patterns of your scars. Pray for the bodies we are. It seems to me the answer lay in thoughts on suffering, to the people left behind in the city, nothing but paradise will do. To the Artist and Poet, it is written, that suffering is part of the human condition. We share it with other human beings.

Depression hears rhetoric and enters the room and spoke fearful reverie, doubt and despair and all synonyms for devouring hope by this dark monster of introspection.

You'll have to live with it for years, feed it so much, it creates a psychic need for new experiences, places, people, let it devours your creative ideas, your poems and paintings, until it has enough and leaves you alone.

Then tomorrow no longer matters, sleep anywhere, as long as there are no walls or roof, sleep on a bamboo mat on the floor. You could add to the story. But their story gets interesting. It illuminates the illusion of a city you lived so many years in. Past comfort, past wealth, falling into mosquito netting and rice with distinction. No money for wine. A woman gave the man five limes and a small bag of sugar.

It is said that golden tortoises swim in Perfume Lake. They surface, bringing luck to anyone fortunate enough to see one. I have seen the preserved remains in a Temple together with a photograph of a tortoise that appeared in the lake five years ago. The Rafetus Leloii is a giant animal. A specimen that died weighed 250kg and was 2.10m long. I have seen the river ripple. I have watched a tortoise surface three times today. I think the Golden Tortoise brings more luck now than I need.

VIII

When I am in my house, my furniture frightens me. AD 2005: Written in blue chalk, under the bridge near the river crossing: Five years out of your home, still I heard a wall of waves, restless nomadic tent, shifting poles in the city. What held the ceiling above us is trust, no truss or nail .This unnatural destruction, why did it happen?

A woman is not a soothsayer. A woman does not look into distances, She does not guess. She knows (to allow space for error). And everything she knew she told the Lover. She told all men until they could no longer hear her. And her voice was (Not) echo, her cry was (Not) wind, but some thing torn from her (terror)The pregnant truth. The full weight of what was. Squatting in the act of birth. The resistance to traction in depth of absence. Too dark to see the crossing you rely on moon (whispered). The measure of all things. The time it takes to recite a creed. The error of a second in a century, was tolerable. An error of this is not some measured resistance to bending of his words. We do not own places we inhabit, these palaces were given to us by another hand. We do not create these places, but during the construction, we find ourselves prisoners of memory.

Only imaginary knowledge, need tools that strike the imagination. You believed the possibility of a vacuum, an illusion of the senses, she said, now correct it by returning to your first thoughts. Who deceives you, your thoughts or yourself? I understand: there are different kinds of understanding. A pencil: draw some conclusions. Our tools are too blunt to touch them accurately. Reach the point, then crush it. Self-interest, the Artist said, it's a marvelous instrument for nicely putting out our eyes. You don't cry ; nerves are martyrised. The war existing between senses and reason is the most powerful cause of error. Old impressions capable of misleading us. The author of graves, wisdom of sage the same as the other. We have many other sources of that error.

Fragments of buttons & clothing revealed this, deeply into the conclusions. Draw permission to observe the fathomless pit of humanity, at the boarders of chaos. Rooster crowing three times at dawn : because it pleased him. Of course, we were left to murder the silence. No doctrine you believe in: no life perfect. Burn your passport: return the ashes to the City. Love is a relic of mine. For imaginary pleasures, after we sleep , we must start all over again.

I am empty-handed, the Artist said.

Without what? I asked.

Rich and expensive things.

I ask you to recall in a photoflash, the world through your eyes. The quality of sight according to one's vision. Ink that made my eyes sting and how we fell burning into the eyes of the sun. Is that how you see things?

I see the wind blowing sand over the face of the sea. The sea is wild and between the waves, foam and spray thickened with rain, beating against the rocks. And the land lifts and carries us, the clouds tearing open rain above us, thrown into the bush and hills, sweeping us with the winds and storms of sand blown up from the sea bed, branches and leaves caught up and shattered, trees bent to the ground, twisting apart and separated from natural growth, like leaves we are torn and tossed in the direction of the winds. And you and I are in some unholy place, sand wrapping around us and I can't see your face for grit, and the wind is dragging you away, your hands over your eyes, and hair and clothes tugged like a fragile paper kite in destructive wind.

126

Reality is adulterated with what you know and what others know and what nobody will ever know, he replied. It depends on your focus. To become aware of what I feel, by trying to create what I feel inside your self, is impossible Private drawings as desolation enters. Black horror doors you were told not to open, Gaelic dorch, the dark doors. The door of fable & fool when you did.

I crossed your threshold. Did I determine my own fate, when I came uninvited? Fate becomes visible on the other side of the door. A threshold is a sacred thing, he said.

Your eyes are the darkest I have seen them. Such a lost expression behind your eyes, as if your thoughts were deserting you. The Artist told me in moments of gray melancholy, falling on the great shoulders of a long afternoon. Come by in the dark side door and share my secret . Stare at shadows of futile sadness. Sweat in this hell, red as fire with me. Or without me. I no longer care, Mané said.

IX

In the narrow room, the floor covered with faded carpets, the floorboards planks of rudely sawn kauri boards, creaking under our feet. Cleaning the floor. Cat walks. You don't chastise the floor – go back and clean again rather than worrying about a few muddy prints.

The windows thick with salt spray, the grass on the lawn tall and neglected. In the upstairs room, two single mattresses pushed together. There is no brush, so beggars dust accumulates in the edges of the room. The pressure of this poverty builds up, like the waves outside the door. I am conscious of little traces of how it was yesterday: the opulent gold famed mirror from another home, the freesias, and the vase on the windowsill. In the kitchen, there are no recipe books. Last night, I baked a berry pie from everything I remembered. There was nothing to add to the memory. We ate in silence.

Looking back at the start of distance between us. When I kissed you just then, distance in atmosphere, like winter following a day of shadows sad ether from the past, like the future I cannot cling to, but I dare not tell you. They are small lies, a woman tells herself, like a flash of lightening, in the middle of the present moment, the womb of a dream. There still exists an unshakeable belief that our dreams mean something, we used to believe that dreams disclose the secrets of the future, or the secrets of the past. I believed in so many things, I imagined possessions for keeping.

She looked at her own image in the mirror, combing her dark hair with her fingers. I have second thoughts about being women or goddess... to be a mother, to be a wife, how all this ends up in a sink of nothing... if you had asked me a year ago, was this possible, had you said what I am saying, I would have told you it was impossible to loose everything. I used to think that destruction was a force of nature, now I am sneaking the world , I ask myself in this reality, fate. What happened? I am reminded of the terrible history we inherited wounds and all cysts and scars and all, with that odor given off by houses, of cooking fat, of mustiness, of a closed bedroom, odor of scars and warm milk, not any sudden grass, gusts of poetry, wild sweeping wind, feathers, leaves, pollen.

But the wound was not my own. Cut deep it comes to this : pointing a finger to the bitterness in your heart, Mané, its full strengthsome call it a tonic following acute suffering. There is a dangerous energy that follows- deadliest recipe with injustice. None were forgiven at the hour of our exile. If you are angry, be angry properly: Don't eat. Don't sleep. Keep anger as a hunger. Stay angry. Angry. Angry. After a while, you will see there is no use in being that way. I feel less sad, I feel quietly sad, I said.

When I spoke to him about the loneliness that closes him down. I saw him standing barefoot. You count shoelessness as the end, the pair waiting by the back door , like genius and destiny, the spit and the glue, beyond first steps you took, beneath your toes, arch, the black dog following at your heels, the last thing on earth we let go of. Shoes. He sat, his feet in the wild grasses, with his hand cupped over his eyes.

What are you doing? I asked.

I am watching heaven, the Artist said.

I could make out the faint vulture of gray days perched a distance away from his tortured heart, I waved my arms and the bird flew, scattering dark thoughts spawned. I made a list torn from memory and I gave the Lover a match and all the flashbacks, filtered and encrusted with all he ever trusted, and the list went on and on, detailed accounts and tiny flakes of chronology, until he understood that he could not do anything. I cannot give any solutions for terrible emotion, I fight against.

There is nothing I can do, to change what was & is changed. I cannot reach a point of acceptance, Mané said, as a priest to crucifix does. Life ripples like a long streamer, stirs in ashes of what was and what wasn't in our lives. Come back with me to the bed-edge, barefoot, no splinters and every touch narcotic, of opium…hot and crazy as a street game.

X

Before, when I sat on a rock, I shook spiders from it first but they were tiny spiders that watch the grass grow , the rocks were soft. You scared me with stories of snakes and spiders. You sketched poison in my mind like a painter , like turpentine in the fir, or a morbid secretion, like a pearl in the oyster, but with words. Everything activates in front of me. But, I was dying my own death, watching you, pulse broken on your wrist. Raw wound of my own thin identity. It was not fate who followed us. Like a sharpened arrow fired from a rusted crossbow. Winding through roses.

(Page of a diary entry concerning leaving)
I noticed the wind died around 3am but the surf is still noisy. In the moonlight, I could see long silhouettes of ibis birds in shredded rag bark of mulberry tree. All the driftwood abandoned on the beach, we collected tiny sticks, the burning camp fire, must have looked from above, like a signal to anyone observing us, here we were, just a pinprick of light on sleeping earth.

In earlier photographs…the photograph of a woman sitting on the grass, dark carbide hair tied tight, red lips, *this lifelong taste he detects in her mouth,* dress floral bouquet, a marriage of wild roses on lilac cotton. Picture the same woman in the photograph shattered. A picture taken later. The past was the whole woman; the future is the broken one. But a woman does not spontaneously unbreak. But it feels like you have.
Even if he kissed her with his eyes shut, given time, we grow like one another. In one photograph, there was a walled garden, I remember

it, the pigeons and peacocks in the white peach tree and purple lavender spikes. Then snow on the ground, a disused brothel as shelter, orange light burning a welcome in window frame. A woman waiting inside. I can never tell whether I am watching you, moving forward or backwards if we are both smiling into the sun,...our faces tanned honey in summer heat.

Both events are possible, the Artist said. Because at the end of the universe, the arrow of time will point backwards, cool objects grow hot, candles will suck up light and living things having begun in the grave will end up in the cradle. Until eventually there is nothing between us, no time at all? Is this happening to **US** ?

The normal direction of time is things growing old and falling apart (I)never (felt) life was slow. Any process that occurs one-way is also permitted to occur in reverse except (something) falling from (a mouth) like shards of glass. Cut us deep. Half and half (again). Tell me the human heart has a memory in fragments, (as) moments from harvested words or things. (Your touch) has in it a love (I know). When you reach out for my hand and squeeze (my heart).

Does it mean (I)hand myself back? And lying (awake) in your arms right (now), the morning light behind the curtains. It is the division of space and time, I am one of the two in this holding together but sometimes I feel myself breaking in half. But I can't begin to tell you that.

There are more ways a heart can be broken than a heart can stay intact. Take this shattered heart. By now you can see the shattered one in two pieces. Or sixteen small pieces, or two big pieces and a lot of china dust. What is it you are saying? Bone shards in the blood. As bright red poem.

When a collection of fragments are hit with a hammer, the fragments break off (fall forward) then will leap back together to form an unbroken heart. There are places where love falls away. We start to climb over them. It is easy to break a heart, in a place where the scar cracks off, difficult, no, impossible to put the pieces back together.

How many ways for a heart to stay intact?

There is one and only one way. If all possibilities are equally likely, it is probable that a heart will go from being unbroken to broken. There are simply more ways it can be broken than unbroken. So fragile the stack of fibrillumn. This heart creaked in its rusty atrium.

The experts called it a point of breaking, as I lay on our double sleeping bag, in this remoteness, away from the city. But there is nothing to cure us. I am hearing lonely in my mind, a sad repetition of sounds over and over, as if something inside me had produced this definitive itinerary and was driving my heart from its anchorage, my heart scratched and tightly closed like a fist I could not open it out and I could feel the bruising and wounding already but there was no way I could prevent myself from leaving in this moment. I am going. I am leaving you. I want the oily waves to drown all words spoken between us. Forever. And that we should be mute and smiling and without the dread of this departing. I wonder in the collision of voices and arguments, how dangerous this separation as we separate out from each other. When two interiors start traversing, you separate. You risk going crazy with loneliness.

It was a primitive flight reflex, I know, but I am powerless to stop this running away, lonely marathon, and I am the only starter in this self imposed exile from all I had known, leaving you and this known love. I begin to see my body's other life. I will read it back, years from now. But, like a lost traveler brought back to life, I will not be the same. I feel my life changes by female intuition.

The year we walk and do not speak. The night we close our eyes but do not sleep. One move in time where light folds like a sheath that holds us. A cloud of tears, the road bent down to find this lost word, like paper lost then found. If we read, if we heard, if the bone fell like rain on the sea of us, shone in the dark like red eye of wolf. In the world a light shone; on the snow reflect white now in the rain land, the night-time comes to us, the wake of sleep, and the wake of dream. But I do not hope to buy this man a gift that the man will escape the pain of life. No more possessions, no chandelier, no mirror of artificial.

Does it matter so much?

I will not try for injustice heavy on us, for what is done is done. And will not be undone while justice lives like an old hermit who is blind but hears and speaks anything.
The body is changed by the motion from moment to moment.

I have now almost made an end, she said.

You told me it would never end, Mané said.

It has no beginning or end. But, something stronger over-rides it. If I leave, will you keep my photograph?

Yes, but an image will not feed my heart, he said. But I will fill my eyes with your face. Hug your shadow constantly in my arms. And by strong imagination, maybe you will become real. Then he pulled me into his arms and into his sorrow. We lose what is certain, while looking for what is uncertain. Trampled fantasies lost on smaller pathways taken towards another end. The vision comes from what is there, in this moment, if you are in a position to see it. I don't have time to see things at close range. I stand for a long time, looking. Then I see myself leaving. See me leaving you. When you undo the rope, I am already gone.

PART VIII

I

Our bodies fall in and out of rhythm. In a lifetime, only a handful of months like this. I left you in winter, but was lost at the farthest places of myself. What will I show you now from a perspective of a thousand days away, from the vantage point of a foreign land. The amber eye of a cat. God exhaling clouds of pilgrims. A rain of silver spoons. A wall of white stone. One body sleeping alone. A column of rusty sunflower- like ghosts of summer that refuse to die. Dark plough lines tattooed in earth.

Along the roads, preserved white phantoms of stone cross, the milky white stones worn down with a pilgrims kiss. A Holy kiss takes a thousand years to fade into the upper margins. In this land are ancient roads and stone markers to tell the distance between market towns. There is a cross outside the gate, six centuries before this. No meat was eaten but on a journey, you were living on almsgiving, allowed to eat whatever you are given.

I wanted you to follow me here. Travel the distance like a pilgrim, each mile cleansing the devils from the past five years until we reach the place where locals place chrysanthemums on iron crosses by the roadside. Surrounded by bright orange flowers and amass of stones heaped at the base. Stones that were built up but over time, moisture softened the mortar. Rust consumed a portion of the filigree cross.

Where was the glittering surface now?

The same thing happens with life, the Pilgrim said. The places of destruction, a razor loses its edge and rust of others destroys parts of you. You can stay here with me and I'll help your life in solitude and celibacy.

While the Pilgrim was talking, she was becoming aware of a bittersweet smell binding her. A fire somewhere, which burned the cold air and left a small lump of charcoal among the embers. The artist's charcoal belonged to Mané. She imagined him lighting a last match and getting a small flame from the charcoal though it was almost extinct. And the fire burned and the flames surrounded them. exploding with showers of sparks, the highest flames making their way into the air and striking the roof of the sky above.

She conceived desire with Mané, the bearing of his children, a long time ago, as her belly swelled with his seed, the richness of a man's seed. She carried it with all of its sap. She bore them with all her strength,... the weight of her beautiful ripe fruit. [Sketch. *Figure seated by the Cross road* with hidden distance.] And she asked herself, what am I doing here, holding these yellow cemetery flowers. The iron memory of the city flattened her, one building rolled over her and cars on the harbor bridge swerved past her, until the streets were empty of everyone she knew. She was partially covered with the dung and dust of it, as it happens when you are leaving a familiar metropolis.

She is made with a mask on her face. She is wounded in the eye by what she sees, she is wounded in the ear by what she hears honey in a mouth and poison left behind. There is no space between. She speaks in glass shards from everything broken inside her. She is thin because of hunger knawing at her heart, she wears a leopards skin... she will change herself, later. She holds a vase in her hands, full of flowers. They are everlasting imaginings or dreams held long enough to gather dust.

She turns her back, as if to eliminate his shadow. There has never been one without the other, pleasures and pain, because they are never usually separated from each other.

136

[The drawing of the woman lighting a candle, painted flame... a breath carries it away] As the figure of an Artist, kissing her. Also his woman, as he slips his hand inside her robe. The fabric holds tiny threads of silk when he undresses her. [With drawing of her].

II

You could ask why she left Mané and went to France. She would not answer you straight away, but make you wait for a reply. It was as an impromptu moment of decision—Fear. Loss. Her illness. Holding three things inside her, she writes these in the journal.[For an allegorical memorandum... as if she trusts herself to forget].When you get to the destination you discover how many things you have forgotten. For necessity? For convenience? I don't know, she answered. The night. A mask. Both hide essential things. How many things held inside you want to forget or is it what you want to remember. From a distance you guess the weather, what clothes you will need, wool, leather. You imagine weather by remembering the feeling of rain on your back, inking its way through green oilskin, to form a cold grid across your shoulders.

Rain that made the common echo of railway station silent, the day I arrived. People stood waiting for the downpour to stop. Whole tracts of air heavily superabundant with the odor of wet sacks and warm tarmac, funky metamorphous rot. The young baker, sweetness of yeasty bread smells, pushing warm baguette into a tunnel of paper bag. He waited. The woman selling magazines & books waited. Even the stray dogs looked scared, waiting in the open doorways. One eyeing me like a tamed wolf set loose from a frontier. The fur with mud. And in the station, which serves as a reservoir of shelter to a stranger, the air of the station is thickly clotted with heavy accents, those places in which sound is mixed up with broad white light. The words hang lost as disparate things touching weakness & fragility. I pass through the crowd of people, one pushes into another, but no one passes through. No map of its immigrants could be drawn up.

But there is a series of images, of vast spaces between us, of the migration back to each other, and the images fall into memory of each moment, and epochs of us that I felt in every fiber.

There were places to go with you… now I have traveled too far away from you, lost from love as if you understood, and the sadness leaks out of my eyes again. They have stolen our palaces, the lakes between our eyes. I am falling asleep on the ice of a deep lake. I am dreaming you are lying next to me but the heat of our bodies makes the ice melt. It was the last of the snow, which melted that winter. [*"Woman at the Crossroads"* 180x 400cm].

Concentrate on a series of drawings that aren't chronologically or logically connected and explained. See this love as a scroll. The intimacy of love, defined by its substance, like water, it has no left or right, high or low. Infinite and unlimited. The text is an open weave. A woman must be loved the way it is felt in the lover. This is called the concentration of loving.

III

(Drafts of a letter [in part] to the Artist concerning absence).

In a farmhouse, thousands of miles from you, I daydream of you in these obscure days. Sometimes with a sense of pain, sometimes with pleasure. If a man is in one's thoughts through the day, I should not have to dream of you at night. But I do. Lying under cold white sheets, the way one shape molds the other. A body of snow on the hills. A plan of a road and river with the words bridge and a description of the land, the names of the nearest village and also the name of the river tributary to the Lot river and the bridge over the river built by a devil twenty kilometers west of the market.

And if it rises above its bank, as it did the year before, it would not be possible to stop the torrent and the village may be destroyed by floods. But you can name a natural disaster. It would not be as bad as unnatural disaster. The way of it, stealth and might, but quietly destroys one man.

The hands, the nails and teeth were the weapons of ancient man. According to Lucrecious, they used as a standard a bunch of grass tied to a pole. These pages are the footprints on the grass. I am absorbing all the moisture with my bare feet. I am taking responsibility for the dew there. I am taking responsiblity for myself.

For a moment I felt your warm body, the weight of you in bed. Even at distance, the memory of you is tattooed on my skin. As I dream you. Dream days before this day. Before this rain, sunshine blue days and the way summer wind blows with sand and long hair

140

is a bundle of warm wheat. He gathers in his hands and ties tight. He tells her love in the morning, while her eyes are half closed, in the light hours before the earth wakes, I heard you, the words whispered low.

On the same page is a sketch or plan of a house showing a room under the living quarters where animals were kept during winter. South side of the house where you smell dampness under years of paint as if the wattle branches holding up three hundred year old walls are sprouting through and come spring, the house will turn into an orchard. These things are possible. The last word refers to the proposition of hope. A belief that things separated can be reunited. There is a faint ghost of passion fruit. Of peach. Peach on a tongue, imagine your body on the blue sofa, the rain falling outside. How do we transcend places to end up in bed with the other in dreams- though thousands of miles apart, I feel you sleeping next to me as strongly as if I turned the light on and you are lying there. Who could see, even if they wanted to, what I am doing.

Autumn leaves falling and on the spur of the hill, stone buildings burnished in the same muddy color. Strange, I can't say how many days passed. The old disturbances had returned and in that state of blackness one can no more tell the days than a blind woman can notice the changes of light.

I close my eyes to see you. We never know which direction we are going, whether we are entering or leaving. Or whether entering isn't leaving at a magnetic point where the compass has no bearing on a past. Even if we swam with compasses, millions of years out of date, we will reach the same lap of shore. Then thunder and the rains start.

I feel that lonely and being alone hold the same weight...So you feel alone. Yes. Alone. I don't want to be alone in the dark. Snow is all around me, a blanket of cold without the comfort of you and a cold symbol of hardship borne of chaos that envelopes us. No matter how well constructed the thought, it is like seeing the structure of a painting, how the Artist can make another world within a world. Sack cloth covering this dead of winter, the hand of God, gravity pushes us like a moon, until we return to the earth and water from where we came.

IV

[We are drawn into Dumas's world through his directness of his work. His are pared down yet it is rich in its sense of place. Even when we do not see any-one physically present in his paintings, there is always a hint of the woman some-where through line or shadow].

Dumas's monotypes are as dramatic as his drawings. But there is not the same kind of tension present. Here work is darker, a more abstract and brooding expo-sition , which recalls the emotional and psychological tension found in the art of Dumas during this period- the years from 2004. One is certain this is not acciden-tal, the drawings from 2005 show the same dark hearted influence. Until there are parts of the Artist, breath, skin, voices, that feel like a stranger. As if you believe the person has suddenly change… nothing subsists, after the people have gone, after the things are broken and scattered, taste and smell alone, more fragile, more immaterial, more persistent, more fruit-ful, remain, remain there for a long time, like souls remembering, wait-ing in the ruins of it all, in a drop of ink, there is no scent to remem-ber a man she has never touched. In a tiny drop… begins the recollec-tions over and over again…closer and hunters' guns shooting wild hare in the distance… how did I get this faraway from you, Mané?

Then come back to me.

No, I have always followed you. It is you who must travel now.

You are stubborn.

Yes.

Then I will wait until you miss me enough. Until you change your mind, Mané said.

But I could fall in love with this place, it's weather, it's life. She sat down and wrote to him. I cannot leave here easily. I promised to look after this place. The house has its own rhythms, its own mistakes, when the roof leaks and the rain comes in. It demands care from me, it is in need of a caretaker, or a God. In return, it is the first place to teach a half-woman (without a man) to find power in herself. I came here with a need for growth, looking for a sense of completion. Do I sacrifice the love to gain this potent self?

The low autumn light enters the far window and settles wasp on the paper as I write. I write in front of the fire. I write while drinking red wine. At times, instead of dinner. I write lying down on the bed under the white embroidered canopy, with small creatures running under the roof tiles above my head. Downstairs cellars for wine and for animals, the pigs, chickens lived below the people. Upstairs one room with fireplace for sleeping and living. Such is the architecture of man and beast.

I made a strange discovery. There are faces in the stones on the chalk walls. Under the poetic illumination, a man embraces a woman. I am seeing so much from the fold of his arm, as close as he is holding her. The stones are set to his obsession and take time to change.

In the living room, eighteenth century furniture, gilt mirror, an empty bird cage with tiny china seed bowls, and on the far wall, a collection of Japanese woodblock lovers. I am curator in this museum, keeper of the key to the carved walnut armoire, with its jars of preserved quinces, fig jam and cognac.

The marbled cat asleep on the blue striped chaise lounge. I am animal keeper to neutered and spayed cats, five laying hens and a handsome rooster. On dusk, I take scraps of bread & fruit down to the orchard. I am the guard who locks the chickens up, saving their necks from marauding foxes. I am the gardener, burying the lemon-wood table under a basket of French roses.

[Notes on layout of guest bedroom]

As you enter, you descend five steps. The narrow molding above the window. Architraves of stone with crosswise markings. The angels carved under. Painted lead white. A small arch, I did not find a secret passage.[With additional notes] An arch is made up of two parts and each one is weak and wants to fall, but one holds the downfall of the other and they are converted into a single strength. A supporting beam between two windows. Pavilion of garden outside the room. Citron trees & oranges & various wild songbirds. Perpetual music and lemon blossom in its weaving.

V

Do you think that somewhere in our genetic memory, you were a shepherd and I, a peasant woman? Building shelter from what was found in the fields: rock, stone, wood. Rough shelter and a fire. You hunting wild things. When we live by the seasons rules, raise children, keep chickens in the basement, pigeons in attics. There was no purpose but to love and survive. The other is contemporary myth. It is the golden egg, treasure chest, Aladdin's cave flying mythical carpet realism and the essential greed funneling into the web of society the Midas touch is illusion and makes us keeper of treasure.

Mané, we need to recognize simplicity, humbleness, and humility. I cannot bear to live as we did before. I want to move away from constant appraisals. From too much consciousness. I am falling in love with this place. It's point of view. Sweeping leaves in the yard. When I heard thousands of fig leaves changing color in the tree, the vine on the wall turning bright pink.

The heart of Mané's art [the woman] is not readily accessible, so in recent drawings his subjects reveal themselves when he creates miniature paintings with a visual language that shows a profound understanding of ink, he narrates the tale of the Artist and a Poet in ink on paper like a storyteller. With a few lines and splashes of primary color, he breathes life into the woman, whose love moves towards him, like a scaffolding, gives back the impossible, takes the viewer from the impersonal to the personal, the Artist who refuses to be carried away by displacement. The phone rings. She answers it.

What are you wearing? he asked. The man is not as absent as she believes.

Lace?

I believe I am enveloped in nothing... a body is not disguised as a thought. He paints, instead, her form and in his mind, a replica of her body. Moving towards each other according to the invisible design, according to memory. I would never dial this up in an insane moment, but imagine now, I am touching you, he said, in a voice expressing his own starvations.

She listens to the deep tenure of his voice. A breathed space between. The power to imagine. It is found in the illusionary. It is found in romantic love, and the creative force. It restores her to a sense of obsession with art and life. Their intimate histories. She doesn't know how this happened. *There is a richly colored detail where one can clearly see the mastery of Dumas's medium. In other paintings, Dumas depicts the conversation between the woman with subjective interpretation, the Artist who understands the physical body, which is often invisible to our eyes, his vision of her, even though we are unconsciously taking everything into our minds, as in Long Distance (2004), portraying the woman in a room he imagines, laying under the silk canopy in room, dreaming a woman is awake.*

There is an irresistible fantasy about his work that is heightened by vivid blues. At this point, a phone echoes and your voice faraway under an ocean. As if the weight of water remembers us. Like a part of my life which has fallen into the sea. Let the dreamers dream, the Artist said. What you call long distance, is the voyage of us. I will transcend all places to be with you. My pathway over the moon. I will come to your bed through lockless doors. I realize there is a physical connection to art and lovers. A creation. Slipping into places my love understood.(I never wanted to leave you)the bedroom where trade winds blew through. To feet barefoot in sand, lime cloth blue water foam. I will slowly undo muscle and skin until the smell of sex lets you in.

(Fragments of a letter to Mané).

By this envelope, distance makes me want... it mutes my desire and I read it, as a delicate envelope, holds a body of words.

Where do you go when you dream? Do you come back to me? Mané asked.

How do you know this isn't a dream? I asked.

VI

There is a first, or early moment, kiss, touch, sex, they stay in the body, stay as a moment which can never be forgotten, which survives inside a deeper moment and feeling, rubs soft and filters through layers and layers of us. Each hour folded like paper in my hands. To hold the feeling, changing as it is in time, we abandon nothing en route, in our private mind, a mind which changes, moment to moment. For without a first moment nothing is worth having, the Artist said.

Taken together one image laid over the other, they will make a book of drawings. An outline of a life observed with care. There is earth in ink, honey in the curve of words in a single stroke. An encoded reporting of what you thought and whether you sleep. By listening to you sleep, I pieced together your dreams, of your secret life. Or awake. Standing naked in your bare bones, you are **older** than other human beings, like the rock drawing of the Magdalenian draughtsman, drawings in the book, pages that were thousands of years old (and its paper made out of rags) I am struggling with many secrets, that are held as words transmuting private agonies , sweet omens of love, stained with the certainty of death, was something rich and strange, with something universal and personal. And I want to be truthful. He is describing an unfinished work.

Some people may, at first sight be disturbed by the lines drawn over this painting as if forming a cage in which the images are trapped. The cage-like structure over the face of the woman suggests a moebius of confession veil with its truth and mystery. More talks later. It is important. I am trying to tell you this… we need to most of all each other, and then figure a way to have a roof and food on the table. You are living the wrong way round. Put love first. Us. And the rest of life can fall into place. Do one thing for me?

Realize now how impermanent everything is, how fragile the moments, how changeable, how temporary, how we take familiarity for permanence, but we by nature are the most impermanent. What makes us remember the hard times as if life is made up of that tiny section of pain. You would see the tears behind this tanned mask.

What are you doing for the rest of your life?

I feel like sleeping through it, he said.

The recorded voice abruptly interrupts. A short message about the problem of connectivity. Her accent heavy. As if you atrophy sensuality and others senses, taste and feel, will follow. The line goes dead, as if the operator cut telecommunications with a simple pair of scissors.

Nights back in my empty room here. I am afraid of empty rooms. Sometimes the roof is filled with sounds of small animals that slip under clay roof tiles above my bed. I sleep, like other woman do who sleep alone. Perishable in solitude a woman sleeping alone, falling inwards into herself; [with drawings, washed in green and sepia, of rivers showing water flowing into inlets... bathed in sweat rivering down her body].

You have seen the woman, I wrote here, her movement and how she moves you. There are other dimensions, thirty-five pages blank, for the woman gives her shape, only when she is being drawn, just as the ink traverses her body and reaches his paper; different textured sketches were presented in his journals, with transparent paper inserted carrying questions that are haunting him.

Dampness in the air, no refuge in the sky where she looks out on ice days into the poetic movement and usual bleak white of winter.

Her figure, such as *Restless and The Horizon,* and *Floating,* explain the distance far from him, even the ocean. From the window the lavender spikes are cannibalized from late summer heat, the weight of snow folding down each crisp lavender cocoon, enslavement like a moth chrysalis the sealed heads show no promise of turning the hills purple in summer and the pollen hives, sweet and nectured liquid turned gold in the alchemist's hive.

Other works, such as Transplanting Rooms are critical comments on this self-induced exile of hers. Yet instead of being sad, Dumas's critique is in symbols or subtle lines, wrapped in heavy charcoal combinations. One shows him placing a miniature house in her hand, while another one floats in between the clouds, a game of balance, of lightness of air, a multitude of small acts, but all deep symbols, in layering of his critique on the exiled or uprooted. He often bought two of everything. A double statement, about vanishing possessions and the impermanence of all material things, including the body.

The painting is one of precise geometry on the picture plane, though in the structure of his woman, a vague line is suggested but it is somewhere else. The eye takes in his use of colors- light blues, faint reds, greens and bluish grays- later the critics would say, his choice of color adds to the sense of alienation despite his carefully constructed scene.

VII

Blue-pinkish hues dominate his paper, often blended with bluish-red and bleeding wounds. But one of his paintings is dominated by red, combined with some white. As if he witness to some rich insight. He pretends to be gazing into the future, vodka in the glass, crystal swans skimming water.

Some days later, people broke into his studio through a skylight and stole the larger artworks. He allowed the rain to fall into the studio. At night he watched the stars.

He does not invite everyone into the seclusion of his studio. A few drawings were placed on the walls. His drawings are influenced by his inspirations, with duplicates of painted images of her face. What was once known as a Mona Lisa look , now presented three dimensionally as if she were becoming a saint, falling back into the renaissance of art, tiny blue beads, a necklace of rain.

The drawings when viewed, are independent works, with the angularity of Cubism, yet, his small drawings on paper, are more suggestive of Surrealism, especially her smile. The watching of a smile being born over and over again, makes me think God sent a plethora of images extracted from one mouth, so that I might finish my painting, Mané said. He is a distant voyeur who sees the woman's face associated with vignettes of memory, a heavy snowfall or the interior of a warm bedroom, close-up and out of focus drawn as they are, together, as if seeking the first lover and second later, inhabiting that thin terrain between memory and reality, visually in one drawing.

VIII

(notes to you from a page of memoranda)

Whatever is natural or voluntary reaches its end by its own accord. If you resist nature then you suffer. For it is said, pain is a malady. Man and woman were born to be happy. When love possesses everything: it makes beauty, happiness, which is everything in this world. All creatures naturally desire to be, he said. When you become weakened, you have to add something new to yourself, new ways of seeing.

You have to add something new to yourself, because no one else keeps creating you. Every effect depends on its cause; the builder makes the house but cement, stones and wood are the form, as if I were on the stairs, walking up through libraries, galleries, millions of people, their casement windows, cherubim fountains. A certain order in order conserves it. Then clouds and sky. The same principle applies to natural things… the cause of the effect only by its becoming.

(Tuesday): Dense fog, like rain. There were two donkeys in a field, shrouded in mist, one had a large tin cowbell around its neck, both eating low thorny branches & twigs from the apple tree. A wild cat under the hedgerow hidden from birds. Cicadas crickets grasshoppers still chirping. A field of dry grass, cocooned in dewy cobwebs. You would not notice the jewels unless the sun was shining. The shimmer they cast could catch the heart.

(Sunday): Sound of wasps in fig tree. The last summer rose grows against white calcium stones, the climbing rose raises the gray scale in its struggle with the stonewall. When you opened the envelope... did a hundred petals fall over your naked skin? Petal & perfume bruised in a letter. I moistened the closure with my tongue. There is fragrant essence of rose falling inside the house, perfume from four hundred years ago, when a rose was first planted and grows there as nothing changes, now in long sequences it continues climbing.

They form the walls landscape with its intensity of distorted forms, color and fresh binding. Discord between pink roses and the colorless wall, between damask perfume and chicken manure. The sound of hunters guns in the distance and hum of cicadas. White shutters and blank pages of a journal. The vases filled with flowers, too many mirrors, too many photographs framed in silver. The footsteps silent.

Outside, I hear the ghost of a shepherd calling his flock. He piles chalk rock on top of rock, he builds a wall through time, chalk & lime & four hundred year later I lean against his structure. As she lies against him. Is it real. Are you real? There is no erasure, no closure. I was not a creator. The ether of man, his name erased in the book of time, yet he still exists *(in the time of sex)*. How 600 million year old amber, liquid sap preserves a butterfly, they examine each tiny wing, pin and label. In my mind, I was listening for the sound of your voice, I was ready to return to you. How human DNA preserves memory and we feel this, *(a Trieste on Heavenly Bodies by Aristotle translated into French)* dream this, imagine. Nothing is extinct, he said. It is only us forgetting what was *(a book about you, which belongs to me)*. To follow the course of the blood, of the wind. I could only hear the thrust of the jet's engines.

There are carnal drawings without an artist, a drawing above earth level, flows wet and painterly, where what we feel is a hand running, following the hand like a painter draws. The hands running over your body, the artist is going over the cadences of her *(the com-*

plete possession). Fingertips hear the body speak. The word for love that slips from my lips, brings us back to a woman dressed in a white-filmy dress with long hair. The woman painted in Dumas's *Night Blindness* with a face similar to her younger self, surrounded by delicate flowers, brushed with obsessive repetition of jasmine.

There are origins in the maze of shadows & fragments, to find your hand leaving its coolness on my forehead. Your face above me. Your eyes looking down into my eyes. The wild part in us. From the pediments of belly. Primitive underbrush, the Artist said. This was developed in the studio known for nude sessions.

Dumas does not wish to abandon his figurative side, they remain open to experiment. His fine nudes are in demand. He does not believe in strict separation of abstract and figurative. The forms of abstract draw from the figurative, for the lines and contours of abstract are in the changing forms of the woman in his life. The broken glass on the table. The blue in his studio has the patina of ancient rooms. It has an odor of the past. He himself looks like a man who was born long ago. Strong and classical.

The paint is peeling from the weight of his thoughts. Some heavy and philosophical, the thoughts come back to him as if they move in a bicameral circle. He spreads out all his brushes on the table. A set of Chinese with carved handles and red symbols on black painted lacquer. He feels restless.

Mané has found a small book , the seed of spatial and temporal beginnings. It is a book of one woman *(from the mouth of witnesses)*. *Dumas does not completely privilege the positive thoughts, to the detriment of the negative to achieve perfection in the book, a lesson from Matisse perhaps. who loves is always in the process of loving.* To love you: to have trust in the other, beyond all proof. It follows the original principle of laying down the transparent layers on the neutral field, in the soft contours, but then the compositions are more infused, overlapping on each other but leaving the outline of each, intact and distinct.

In love, know the genii of another. Every scar inscribed, every dance to the edge, like the stars you invented, drive without stopping. The fire that spreads and all its teeth are flames, *(seven hundred thousand volumes… all of the books burning in the siege)* the memory of spices fills the room cinnamon, women you loved with love or without passion, *(the translation must have been in ink)* I hear the women embracing him in the dances of beings .The woman he held once and will never meet again.

IX

Dumas's artistic impulse moves towards calligraphy, some of his works borrow from the organic abstract of early cave paintings. As in Black Monochrome (2006) he does away with contour lines, but relies on the spiritual energy released from a white background, Dumas uses broad brush strokes that may transverse into the air, strong brushed lines that seem to fly into the figurative. Into the air.

For the Poet has been collecting invisible information, an imagined idea of place and experience, as air collected in silk bags. A poetic gesture originally inspired by Marcel Duchamp's *Air of Paris.*. From the air samples, she can tell the direction of the wind and temperature of the day. *Of Air,* four handcrafted books contain transparent figures on an opaque background. When the pages are turned the first image undergoes a metamorphous as if the translucent layers of her are seen in depth, touching and overlapping, imbued in the books by means of exquisite control.

A style that is entirely Dumas's, consists of black fruit & organic forms reminiscent of forests & flowers. Often these appear and disappear in Dumas's paintings. Branches of fig leaves embracing the lovers in summers, these subtle *sotto voce* works hide forms and details, lying between the figurative and abstract, as they will fade in showers of falling leaves-strength and beauty amidst fragile impermanence, often equated with the human spirit.

And I smell the fig wood of his fire. A fire keeps him warm until his woman. returns. When the evening fog cloaked us both in white, *(Virgil says that the shield was white , formed by the painter of shields, and these were formed by bones bound together, made smooth with rubbing)* I did not ask

157

Can you see me ? But: What do you see?

The ghost of the shepherd answers. I see the soul of you carried by angels into the gate of the moon, he said. Birds of dreams. A man who sees such a vision looking into my eyes and listening in the mist. He listens to voice in the fullness of her earth. Reading primitive signs on the body: It is physical form & positions begin and end with him, a passage through animal & vegetal, by the roots, the seed, the fruit, leaf, skin of him, into the garden inside us.

At the reversal point, the desire and descent of you into me, of me into you. The rooms we inhabited, Mané, the secret of two co-existing. It is only in the act of love that we are in the present. As he loved my body under a quilt embroidered with trailing tendrils and oak leaves. Later, I remember his hands as he peeled mango. Taste, he said and slipped a lozenge in my mouth. Slowly he followed the journey his finger had taken , tracing my throat with his tongue. Skin on skin perfume, kisses mouth, half-open, tasting lips of crushed violets, prolonged kiss, feeling the curve of his cheek on belly. I wrapped my thighs around him, flushed with touch and I loved in innocence as warm beneath crewel branches, embroidered where birds of paradise hover and Chinese figures stand guard outside lemonwood pagodas. Linen thread on raw silk into garlands of bridal buds that weren't quite open. Let me lie with you, this place is silent and the earth feels warm. Let us stay in the garden and be lovers in the leaves. And while my skin was still moist from loves libidinous pleasure, he draws the quilt around my body. I peel back the edges. You imagined love's scene, always the same folds of the quilt, the way sepia light threw warm shadows down the wall in a stranger's house, the man speaking with a foreign accent, as she was a foreigner. And he draws me on canvas, then paints me with oils, covering the woman's body in silk quilt while her skin still moist.

He promises to call again. And he does. They all do. Such is the connection, in dreams, in daydreams, I have always seen things this way. Duplicate worlds would have some degree of blurring. The blurring might be too small to matter or it might be so bad that the copy would be unrecognizable. Like a newspaper that has been screened too many times, like the sound of your voice on a long distance call. Some connection from the past, they were once all her lovers, this is what she feels, that at times she "remembers" all men from another time, as if the human heart has memory. Your Virgin? Your Model? Your Lover? I am all these women. Yet when I write our past, I am another woman.

Every correlation between two people is given away and found. Yet none are visible to the naked eye, Something breaks through when you touch for the first time. You fall in love outward, as if in the falling, pulse, sweat and blood are similar weight. One moment more, a kiss on a mouth, when you transcribe feelings with lips, the tongue's wet syllables, pressure of your mouth. Soft stabs punctuate text of kiss. One moment more, a night of discovery, close connubial sweat, yet it is just the beginning, I could love you, if you let me, the stranger said (learn multiplication from a kiss). Slow dancing, grinding our bones together: in the dream of another life. And then he asked in a tongue that was foreign. I turn my head. All I could think about was you.

X

Dumas refuses to call his exhibition retrospective, though his critics do. He prefers to call it an inventory, which he does once every three years to take stock of his own production. There is nothing left that can be taken. Invisible money was bent by others deceits, subterfuge and treacheries, plundering your possessions of living inhabitants. Your blood felt the impact, it can be reached by cruel knives. It can happen on a year like this, the lack of sleep before a life-changing event. You could hear human souls making plans under ground, when they became black and heavy, you could not distinguish them from iron or stone.

Then, too, it's opening in Hanoi, marks the new life he makes here, despite the crowds of people living in the streets, the brick dust, humidity and heat.

The art of Dumas had to do first with his relationship, with the Poet, they wrote, and later, the definition of his identity and the positioning of his artistic personality in the midst of personal loss and subsequent poverty.

The later linear work 2000-2005 Terror Firma (2003) and The First and Last Judgment (2004) show this preoccupation with aligning, realigning, shifting away from social rules and structure. In Torn Shirt (2006) options, attitudes, relationships as he depicts his own shirt, as if torn from his back, the fabric gesso and embedded paper , in black charcoal lines rendered without identifying signs of its material or human past to become its own entity, a passive subject , a dark shirt with a ghostly omnipresence pulling him out as if subjected forever to passing forces.

In this work, Dumas appears to have made himself personally responsible for the fate of every human being who views his art.

EXTRACTS FROM
THE ARTIST'S LETTERS

1. I was left with the impression of oblique pathways or ridges of a cliff, soldiers moving through a field, the origins of simple mechanical process disrupted by erasures, the rupture broke the surface into facets of memory. I did not want to say goodbye. I wanted to be leaving with you. Terminal is a word for an ending. I felt you inside my body and couldn't leave until you had flown. I couldn't drive out of the car park until the tears had stopped. I waited a long time.

2. So the summer left, you left, and I could capture neither one. How could I hold the strings of days with you- in the warm waves, crumpling themselves against the islands of our naked bodies. Or in the patterns of light cast on your face, under the memory of noon-lantern of mangoes, on the sand that stretched from the headland at Alexander Bay to the grooves of paper -bark trees, their branches traced on the ancient tablet of blue sky? Will these things remain...like the piles of sad bleached bones, undistinguishable as human or animal, they are used as a marker for every passerby in the desert,...there are no signs of a fading.

3. I found the card and a photograph of you - to remind me, as I write this, it has already happened. Like the seeds of the past, folded in a letter, tiny, fertile endearments, sown word for word, made explicit and private, by years of sex with you. And I can see you on the beach, (descriptions of this morning) held as complex

drawings in my mind, which overreaches the artist's hand. You are so beautiful.

4. If I could remove the months following your departure, I would take away three months that followed it. The rain. Often in the night room, the rain followed more rain in the diary of grief, each night turning into torrential downpour, my eyes wet by morning. I was drowning. I ached with this sense of departure. Its scenario implicates me to a tragic script, devised by a sadist somewhere else. By the unbearable details, it feels like death reversed... it comes curving in, this pain of sadness as if uncovered from the despair of all mankind, it comes to me without rehearsal, to fall into a deep well, the pit of earth, its heavy damp contains all the spores and seeds of all earths sorrows.

5. So many memories of you today – for this room is the last place we were together. The tangerine pareo I tied to branches above the tree. It was wide enough for a roof. It turned your body the color of ripe citrus. Now your mouth tastes of oranges and wine. This private room was the last place we indulged in our taste for sex. The intensity only made me more acutely aware of the love I have for you. 48 hours after you left. I'm sleeping in the room. I'm painting *Without.* (cold-pressed paper and ink). For you signifies love, which is both visible and invisible, hiding us both. I am the masked artist, by some fated maneuver, both the apostles and Judas as myself. Bed pushed to the side, tangerine tarp at the foot of the bed to protect from blue splashes. Canvas drop by the door. So much plastic I am sleeping in a crime scene, so much canvas, sleeping in a tent.

6. My moments are filled with you and I have not stopped thinking about you for a single moment. Everything that belonged to you the space of you absence in the bed, during the night , your absence reminds me that I am still here, I miss the weight of you on the other side, scent of you still on my skin. A lover should take these things

with you when you leave. You are coming and going from me. There is sadness in the coming and going. When I walk back through the door, it is your face I want to see first. Come back to me.

7. Picked a volume of jasmine, Not a day passes that something does not happen to remind me of you. Of you and me in our nature moments.

8. In bed again where you usually sleep. Of beautiful breasts, thighs, eyes, arms to hold and fingers to caress, toes to touch and hair to twist and ravel. In that house, we used to sit on the veranda facing the sea and watch the sun falling behind the sugar refinery, the hill with its wall of green bush, the red ribbons of sky; watch the day burning out, the painted wooden houses endangered by the blazing sky.

9. Stood under the outdoor shower in rain, dripping into the grass. Green solitude of the gardens, the variegated leaves the criss-crossing spiders intercepting pathways of sticky juice, the height of the rainforest enclosure. Something moist I remember about collecting liquid in the leaves with you. As if the tropical, the hibiscus flower, the Venus orchid, and giant trumpet flower can devour a man with her nocturnal scent.

10. (Fragment of letter written on Sunday). When you have limited time, it is amazing how the situation becomes more focused. The sun feels more luxurious, the crickets sing more and the evening air so balmy and then the mosquitoes. The metallic hum of mosquitoes, the living velvet of iridescent butterflies, all of it he wrote, returns me to living, reminds me of life, which had been flickering in a wind.

11. I found my envelopes. I haven't heard from you. So I am worried about you. Can you blame me? I can't help it. I ache when

you are sad. It's my nature. You had left two incisions. One horizontal scar left by a knife which escaped from my hand, when no one was there to hold it for me, the other this pale slash on a mouth, a smile before you told me you were leaving. Another wound I feel. But it is said, each heart receives a great burning scar that stays as part of you.

12. You know that I shuffle between diligence and obsession producing blessing or curse and act of genius or infirmity. Letters are a sign that I am alive, my sentences, some proof of human existence... but a combination of writing to self, writing alone, telling to a mirror of self, you are my audience in this lonely play... and I think survival is in trust, to allow us to find each other again. I imagine a fine thread, like silver thin gossamer that wraps from you to me.

13. Went to the store to get green beans. Because I had no sandals, I walked barefoot. Warm linoleum, nobody gave me a second look.

14. I am writing this in bed with the green pareo draped over the pillow next to me. As you left it. Love you so much. Off to sleep. I will write when I am settled so you can have a stack of love letters to carry around.

15. I walked into the city market in shorts and tee shirt with a large flax bag over my shoulder. Caught my reflection and wondered who I was.

16. I am going to be alone here in half an hour. I want to kiss you on the mouth and feel your body against mine. I am sick of thinking. I long to splash your green pareo and make it cling to your brown legs. I'm trying to stay in the moment my mind racing ahead of days, weeks, and years. Guessing and desperately trying to find a pattern to move towards. Without a pattern, the mind lurches like an old wood-

en cart pulled by a donkey. I am not sure if I am the cart, the donkey or both.

17. I visited a painter today. He paints scenes of backyards in the city. Gardens without people. Parks of vacancy. I told him it feels like someone is buried there of tapu land Some ominous feeling, I said. His eyes light up. Yes, yes, don't they.

18. Love you sexy lady. Love you long time. I am feeling pressured by the amount of letters winging their way from the hand of my lover. I will write again soon, probably tomorrow. I might get some beautiful envelopes so you know the letters are from me. It could be the French series or something. In my mind, I am following you around the world.

19. I visualize your every look and your body, to know someone so intimately. That you can be with them anywhere. I was visualizing you for other purposes. Carnal. When we get back together, you better be fit. I am never going to let you alone for at least a week. No interruptions. Just food, wine, maybe some coffee. One last envelope, and the last of the stamps.

20. Monsoon rain tonight I am really missing your person in my life. I feel two-dimensional.

21. Ears are cochlea shells. The tiny bones broken.
Lately I can't hear what people say, the sound of ocean in my ears, but what they say does not matter. Only your words. Come back so I can hear the sound of your voice.

Dumas paints in a spontaneous process. Similar to his approach to the unbroken line, Dumas works directly with the material. For him, making studies are not necessary, instead of a subtractive process in carving, he builds up layers of paint to achieve texture, color intensity and depth. Another element that identi-

fies these paintings from this time during the woman's absence for his life, is the inclusion of inscriptions and fragments of letters within the picture plane. Handwritten, almost calligraphic in its own right, each piece compliments the painterly brushwork. Placed in different positions, these black linear strokes seem to complete the whole composition.

Still life. A metaphor for this life is a large-sized work, with darkness similar to working in stone. He relates that although the black looks cold, the brush strokes create warmth, an intimate relationship with the ink. The large paper allows him contact with the surface and ink, creating intimacy with the medium. Lovers' dialogue, lips and fingers, conceived moment of desire, revealed by light from the fire reflected on iron with cherubs and someone's initials. Renaissance date in Roman numerals, wrought iron leaves and honeysuckle flowers. His *Still Life* contains the quality of rawness alluding to the idea that the vulnerability of the aesthetic object, by inherent nature, is fragile, there were scars from embers, burns from candle wax, and deep scratches from cutting bread and hard cheese on the table. Out of the wine, the Grenache caught in his glass, like red flames on his tongue. Then inking the blood, to a heart's calligraphy, he returned to wait for her at Villa Hanoi.

EXTRACTS FROM THE
WOMAN'S LETTERS

I

And so there are the letters, yours and mine, and I opened what I knew, messages from beyond love's boarders. Pilgrims' came here by instinct- I was pushed by losses. After the first letter, I could not do anything but think about you, by the time I answered, I saw you enter my dreams. I am absent because I am the dreamer. Only you are real.

The moment, I wrote you all those months ago, as I was looking through St Augustine's Confessions, I randomly selected passages and browsing through old architectural books, I cut illustrations of types of vaulted ceilings, (groin and covered vaulting), tools and systems of precise measurements, rulers and calipers; then plotted the images and words together, arriving at different permutations, set these on white paper, in a letter to you, to send manmade structure and thematic psalms from a Saint, who, seeing into his own mind and finding truth in every thought, suggests true essence and eternal qualities, based on his own understanding of inner nature. The words remind us of pools- still, but not stagnant, enriched with the passing of time.

Letter by letter, your lips are the seal on the back of the envelope. I could detect where your lips licked the glue and your fingers pushing across the seam. It holds the secrets and protects the opening. Each letter contains the inventory of a late summer. You sent roses (when you open the envelope, do not bruise the petals). When you read the words, use them against me. Then you sent winter jasmine, the flowers faintly there. And a cherry stone I sucked for a short time and the pips fell on the path. And this happened so many times on my sojourn to the letterbox, an orchard of cherry trees grew.

I recognized Vietnamese stamps, the curve of your capital letters, envelopes often soaked by the rain. There burns the pattern of existence, loss of time, loss of my shiny gold rings and silver bells, tell me I can change places with Jesus, reclining half naked, pale stretched out among fern and butterfly orchid, the true brother of each thing and every secret, asleep in some corner or envelope.

I sent miniature verses from Saint Augustine, my mind rests there in the rivers of his book. It is broken in parts like afternoon shadows. Like male and woman shadows, lying side by side, one stretched after another, who through their love, across the edge of centuries became the Lovers that other lovers followed and all the prophets followed. The pilgrims lost and found again, walking about on the different roads of the world.

I tore the corner of blue wallpaper, gold heraldry, and I, traced the circumference of a fig leaf, sent the feathers of pigeon, the wing of a blue meadow butterfly, yellow petals from tiny chrysanthemums, the churchyard ones and French lavender from bee garden of honey hives.

As rain will drown the bees and one steals honey they left behind for our toast. The bees that made wax for our bedroom candles. They gave us light. Still we forget them.

What was it you wanted back then?

We knew what we wanted from each other, it was more than I could write, the Artist said. Your hair wet, you were standing at the entrance of my door – when you left I began to forget the sound of your voice, it fell into vacant spaces we left, the curves of your body fading until I was looking back into silence. There are photographs of you... the image of you vanished into the image, like paper passed beyond conscience and for a long time you will not return - that image is faded.

Friends' asked me: why are you sad. It was the wine. Many grapes. Wine makes me speak about the man, I knew, the hours, the light of time, it burns like a log and the wine, though at times my mouth opened as I tasted old sadness, old works worn out and destroyed, but afterwards, in the aftermath of what it was I remembered, it became foreign, to look back on our lives and cry again and whisper what was lost, the fire warm until the words I say to a stranger become filtered through truth.

What happened to the letters I sent you, Mané asked.

Your letters had an unfinished quality. This does not mean fragmented, but a feeling that they were incomplete.

So, where do you keep incomplete things?

I keep them folded up in my intimate drawer, silk and satin tracery. I left still in love with you and the loving does not fade, but gets stronger. I still find myself falling deep into your beautiful words. First, I tried to forget you, I've tried not to obsess about you but I think about you. I haven't forgotten you. I miss you. Already on the folds traces of pen. You should know your words engulf this whole woman, before I read it. I inhaled the summer perfume of salt on your skin. I read through and the story makes me think of you & warm ghosts of coral seas, when we swam without thinking, water entering our mouth, fusing a smile on your face, bursting into ecstasy.

This intimacy goes further. And it does. Your letters are fragments of ocean, dense blue, leaves me wondering how you wrote a poem on it. There are no books in the sea, but the waves remember us, the water opens its arms to wake us, the swimmers lying in bright water. I taste saltwater as iodine carried with us from infinite ocean, magnesium of invisible truths, and there you wait, squinting in the strong brew of sun, standing up to your shoulders in blue mosaic.

I made an [etching of words] with small fishes and floating island on cotton paper. I could not tell if it was jute sacking, sugarcane, banana, rice, straw, tea or pond algae. But when I printed the island, the fiber laid a surface pattern of sand. Then we found an unlived corner of the sand, shared mango sherbet vivid snow in sugar cone melting down to your elbow, then wrists. This life essence we conjured up between us... does it remain like rare perfume in the room of soul. As lips pressed to my lips leaving me with sensual hunger to suddenly touch you. Touch your skin and I sense what is written there, the more I touch your skin, the more I feel.

My long and frequent letters remind me of certain papers we tied to kites with string a long time ago, we called them messengers; some of them the wind used to blow away, others were torn by the string, and a few of them blew up and stuck to the kite. These letters, my present messengers will stick to you like a moments rune or charm, to unriddle surface meanings, then the secondary underpinnings of the words that compose it, and these two patterns are in dissolvable, indestructible and one. This house is filled with the photographs of immigrants & farmers & peasants, a family in a house. In a black & white photograph, a man who looks like you, he is standing with a woman holding his son. Why does every picture remind me of you?

Within the intimate confinements of his paper, Dumas's drawings are clearly influenced by her absence. He seeks respite through romantic compositions. Amorous themes and female form translated onto a white surface. Dumas's use of stark colour contrasts-red on black, black on white; and black on gold, the woman's red dress-blurring the boundaries between her body and the background. Through the sensual body language, her hair falling off her right shoulder, she turns around and looks at him.

When he frames it, the Artist avoids hanging it at eye level. Instead he presents it on the floor propped up against the gallery wall in a continuous series of ten large copies along an entire wall. The atmospheric portrayal of the lovers infuses a distant mood, again a transference for his mental state at the time, the image of the lovers together, with traces of love still there, yet minus her presence, this work, the critics wrote, is an obvious analogy to reality, illusion ,the body supposed to be a complimentary take on sexual desire and coupling. While beautifully stimulating, all ten prints offer, instead, an immediate connection to the unpredictable, and uncontrollable nature of human emotions. Although not obvious, the work feels abandoned.

The second, a painting in acrylic on paper, Between Love and Structure, was inspired by photographs Dumas took of her in student days- an art magazine. He recently discovered these black and white negatives. More than the seventeen year olds nakedness he remembered, it was the sense of being with her in the room, its sparseness, and random choice of objects that attracted Dumas then, as now.

Developing an image of her in the past, beautifully profane, finite, linear photograph of fallen angels, and the third solo exhibition for the artist when he was younger. Influenced by 19th century erotic illustrations, *Dumas objectified photographs, focusing on her bare body and her hair tied loosely with satin ribbon, the room full of symbolism, candles, apples and arrows.* You were seventeen in the photograph, lying across your double bed.

In the photograph of the girl reading, she is ignoring the camera eye watching her, the artist standing behind the camera holding her image. There is no single way to see everything. There is just a desire to connect. The monochrome flatness of the paper is interrupted only by the suggestive entry of red. I keep the photograph of you next to my bed. how young were you then and how beautiful: he said. Your image is the last image I see before falling asleep.

I look at the photographs. I want to look back to our origins. To the beginning of us. Photographs of you taken from different angles. Then negatives at the outline of something else. Other loves appear and disappear, the more you love you take, the more secrets you hold. But later, love has an ingrown quality. Slowly, we became part owners of each other.

THE ARTIST AT VILLA HANOI

Mané's life became a temporary camp in the rooms of many. Anyone who came in saw the suitcases, books; and drawings rolled up. There was always a bed unmade and a rainbow of silk shirts crumpled in the corner. There was always thought of moving out of the villa, and coming to see her, of going to places never traveled to. In a room of fragrant yellow roses in the Chinese jar, dominated the room with damask perfume. Hidden far back, the china of many broken dreams tossed at your feet. Anyone who saw you, left poorer.

The sound two gates roughened by distance. Two things closed at once. And all the while, you were moving through this land of poetry, as the silk and brassy feathers of dead roosters, on the bicycles of the women. In the city the building daily breaking under pick axe and hammer, dust falls inside lungs and on the window ledge of the villa. The air thick with smoke and brick dust. This was his Hanoi.

In the French colonial villa, there was an artist's studio and one large bedroom. It was easy lying there in a room away from the street. Sometimes he could feel the edges of her sweetly embalmed in the corners of the room, yes, she had left everything, her books, her clothes; she had taken a handful of blue days on the horizon to follow, his words held in place and sometimes if she had stayed longer just to hear the timbre of his voice. I am no dream interpreter, but there will be no other, woman in my life, the Artist said. But she left before he could tell her.

The room had high ceilings and tall doors and you kept looking at this, but in that room, your eyes could not adjust to the distance

between the floor and the ceiling. The room was not one they painted, the pale yellow walls and green deco ceiling fan.

There was a desk on one wall, a dresser with woven water lily
drawers, shared, clothes she left behind, his clothes were closer to the
mosaic floor and dust blown in from the street. Sheets dried on the
line strung between the two villas had flakes of gray paper ash from
offerings, always the odor of burnt money, when you changed the
sheets. It was hard to keep things white.

The room had an air of tranquility and coolness from gentle
breezes, unlike the other rooms which were at the front of the house
and the noise from the cat on heat, cages of songbirds in chorus, a
hammer from a man working in a nearby building and women with
bamboo baskets, looking skywards and calling for residents to buy...
warm rice and peanuts in a banana leaf wrapper tied with twine, fresh
baked loaves of bread, always the same cigar shape, tiny plastic coat-
ed remnant of wire.

There was a fireplace in there with photographs of family on the
mantle, a beautiful family, in delicate days before the harsh, beaten
years that invaded them later on.

Around this time, the thunder rolls in after a day of heat.
Cracking over the clay tile roof. White lightening flashed in a full
light that light up the houses. You used to watch the rain change the
peach and melon of painted houses and the smell of rain and lime-
wash. The storms occupy a place deep inside you. They are still
with you.

When the rains fell, the shutters wet, managed to look freshly
painted. The roof was layered in clay tiles with a lightening rod
shaped like a crane bird, the gutters and down pipes were half rusted ruins and a chimney bricked up, and holes for brooding pigeons,
resembled the roof of a château, the ancient well in the courtyard
filled up with culinary herbs, mint and sacred basil and in parts overgrown with weeds, From the entrance to the kitchen, the floor was
covered in black and white tiles with Grecian edges... the whole

floor looked like a ceramic chessboard. The living room had high ceilings and six full length French doors that open to the street, separated by a waist high lattice trellis, covered in branching vines of purple bougainvillea and on terrace, giant blue and white china pots with miniature frangipani trees, bonsai size decorated with gold charms hanging on red ribbons to bring luck.

The furnishings in the living room are rattan, including the table, which is covered in English newspapers, and the books in the late 19th century bureau are Asian history and folktales and travel magazines. And the ceiling fans that are left constantly on, are all rattan & wooden. There was a briefcase on the chair, a camera, an orange pareo draped on the back of a sofa like a shawl. Still prevalent are the fabric backdrops, the patterned silk that lend a deliberate Oriental quality to his erotic, naked portraits, the flat cloth accentuates the skin, the florals that back the skin bare poses are overstated compared with the usual white background, his hand draws his model, traversing around her breasts, his brush comes alive in this carnal dreamscape and the effect is beautiful. The fibers of animal brush conjure up a feel of her hair, with his hands running through it. The exquisite balance between movement and stillness, the slow repetition motion of the fingers- that move without really going anywhere. The works probably are, as the press release suggestions, ruminations on themes. No one but her would remember or understand.

In the villa, Mané spent afternoons, looking down into the alley. Sometimes watching rats run across the woodpile, through shattered green shutters and broken teak table, the bentwood chair with three legs and a hole in the woven rush seat. For every rat, there were cats & kittens, young cats following a skinny mother cat, watching how she separated chicken bones and boiled fat from plastic lids with her teeth, she looses herself in the bucket of garbage. The cooking pot simmering lone spine bone and snout of a pig. There were chili and lime and fermented squid, purple basil & lemongrass & tamarind floating in soup.

Unlike the rooms facing the street, the bedroom window looks out across the tamarind tree avenues, shrine gardens and a temple which lead to an orange lacquer bridge which rose elegantly in the middle like a tiny hump and reached an island with a four story pagoda, like a miniature carved house with a hundred arched windows , where the red sun rose behind, until the perfumed pagoda shrine glowed pink in the mint green water. It is said that an Emperor dreamed of a lotus shaped temple in the center of a lily pond. On the advice of wise woman, he built it and shortly afterwards his woman gave birth. It is supported by a single pillar with a brick and stone staircase running up one side.

The pagoda symbolizes the pure lotus sprouting from the sea of sorrow. I have seen dragons run on the apex of the curved tile roof. Monsoon rain is falling in the streets, turning the cumquat paint on the building a deeper shade of yellow. It is said that the Gods came down from heaven to play with women here. They created a woman and she spoke to him.

There were other bones, in the archeology of the remaining dream, civilization was in the wilderness, crumbling walls, forlorn bridges, rocky balustrades and gateways, mysterious flights of steps falling through the hole in the sky. He would listen as the breaking apart of the timber fell towards him. To survive he must run away from the house as the beams fall and intersect the physical. A jungle of trees entangled with lianas, early morning mist and cloud slowly burn off as the sun rises and the forest comes alive with the sound of birdcall, animal cries and the humming of insects. He heard them one night. Before dreams when all spirits are returning from bones buried at the base of silence.

In the streets, the Vietnamese women selling melons and bread early morning, now shelter under blue plastic shop awnings in the rain. From the back of brick courtyards, the smell of pork belly barbequed over coal fires burning in second-hand ammunition cans.

I am painting on the shroud of a Jesus, stretched over the bones of my own image, he said.

In the artwork, each line is a gash of paint, linseed and turpentine mixed up depth. Under them, the white canvas is translucent. His lines are both visible and invisible, hiding his identity as people know it and visible, in which claims his unique self as he defies the gray conformity of the people around him.

His works at this time alternate between the linear and painterly with a handling of tone that exude an atmosphere of time and place, even their different titles refer to referents or events in the real world. *Woman missing (2004)* captures the loss of the woman in red backgrounds of the orient, lines of black, then white as a relief or white ghost form, an important part of his *oeuvre*.

He draws a thick darkness shared by seven million people, he had experienced too much, the smell of mould, a rot outside to match the rot on the inside, its dead sensation to sublimate his love of her, a thick darkness of the heart in hotel lights, still slings to his memory. His mind allows the poison to taint what he see, undiluted for this dark air to permeate the structure, until the bones are knitted in black. He was immersed so deep in her and found he could not go back. Now the picture of this woman joins with the paint and the sound of frangipane growing. There are hundreds of flowers to pick and thread into a necklace.

You can sense the woman, the Artist said. I will not be detailed in the telling but leave a gap in the years. Some months were nothing but repetition. I can find it now. I leave it somewhere in the painting, repetition…repetition in tight fold across the sheets when the bed was made. The sheet pulls back from the same bed. The bed's white snow over a hill of bodies.

You can smell the woman. She seeps through between the guild and illumination. She has come to cover all the shadows with her perfume. Such a work on Arches paper, painted with red ink, a parodic image of the woman, for the commemoration of de-*saparecidos (the disappeared)* with its luminous ghostly effects including the soul. She is inside now.

Slowly, oriental colors attracted his eyes to the sweet manifest saffron and pink orchid blessed by poverty by the artist who knew and understood some slim barrier between poverty, he calls it a line... what line reminds him knocking on the door of humanity, what it meant in the event of a boarder crossing, once when he watched a woman tossing coins, he asked her why she was throwing money, into water. So I can return here, she said. Coins thrown in a lake. When children are hungry. It is a waste, he said. And lately, the sound of women's voices, among green rice... he is writing this note on the smooth side of rice paper. They call rice paper, the field of the artist.

Despite his use of black ink, Dumas has not given up painting in colour. In the past year, he came up with two important works. The first, consisting of a landscape canvas. For an artist, trying to make sense of his feeling for this life, he became desperate. The paint dries on his canvas and between dark spaces we stand squarely on the earth , the space opens out, classical, ordered, unordered, 1923 lines , their intersections have domes shaped like enigmatic pagodas, red spurs of lacquer bridges, rice paddy fields of emerald shoots, ethereal blue gardens spread out like a diadems of a palace in an infinite maze , makes itself deep and permanent. From it, the Artist scrapes memory. His new works are less disturbing in mood [than many past works] allowing Mané to play around with formal elements as he did in the 1980's.

One quality that links his early works with the new series is his desire to create a personal footprint. He discovers the linearity and flatness of the image and composition. I want to take possession of everything that exists. I am not looking for you, I am you, he said.

When I am gone, you paint me into your own self- portrait, (when you represent me, be honest in what you portray, note that my skin is paler and lines around my eyes are deeper) it was nothing but a simple line (I had not seen before), surrounded by the shadow of a man made by sun cast on a wall, (yet it represented all the incidents of the scene) the branches of ribs, the faded banks of a smile, the river between, (green eyes reveal true color- saturated moss) and if you were to ask me about the point of sight, the sad painting when you look back to a time of most resistance (the figure broken and confused by too many lines) I would ask you to make another, and another, until you represent us as angels or saints in another time. Or portray us as pilgrims, (but not to many to cause a crowd) when you set us together in the foreground and keep us in view, (legs bent at the knees when we are kneeling down) a larger scale perhaps and then by diminishing the past, make the clouds thinner so the true color of our sky is seen through, where the line of vision sees a road taken (as nothing) disappearing into the distance, make a gate (held by my hand in your hand) and close behind us, (lock it as you draw it).

Make us larger than before (feet parallel and separated from another) the sad road behind us (the shoulders leaning forward) make the trees large, birds, clouds and similar things in our world, (thighs rubbing) put us back together (arms folded) then we made another shadow (passionate strokes) on the curtains velvet ravine, (legs apart) and when I reached to touch you, the branches cracking and falling into the river, you hold tight, (the natural position is pushing forward) the way we move into each other (quickening movements). Sex, (clandestine) voyeur of this night, you have seen this before, for I have seen you writing obscenities as another book, I don't care for decorum (neither do you), pray for us, that we live to split this fresh warm bake of holy bread (no confirmation needed or accepted) toast it in the morning, high altitude coffee and guava jam, (sanctify), Holy, Holy, blessed by them (for they) take the money, touched and held in the palm of every saint. Another day passes by us. Who represents this muddy track, this divine pathway (sees us holding hands again)... lipstick and black mascara cleansed from a face (angel & dreamer) before she sleeps.

Current life… there needn't be a separation between writing a narrative and your experience of current life. A desire to take what was left, begin life with him and do everything right. this time. While not appearing to be plot driven in the sense of events leading one to another, but you may be attempting to give the sensations of this, you could deliberately write a slice of life that is non climactic with no epiphany yet is rich in perception and image. Where your life is in the present with so many things happening around you. So you create a living memoir. This IS what is happening in your life. This metaphysical element- of assessing writing on that page while writing- can add a dimension of honesty and total engagement of the writer.

Mané found the words on a simple note, written on both sides of the paper, lyrical & tragic & transient, he felt her so close, so clearly, the weight of her life as she looked back over her shoulder. He took his hands away from his eyes so he would see what it would be. He saw her beautiful eyes. So close that he could detect a level of water rising in the corners and the color green, he would identify her with for the rest of his life. She had followed him through so many addresses.

You have reached me amongst the dreams… from the debris of your life and my life, already a promise is emerging. It was on the last day of September before the month falls into October, when I decided to return.

Step back into your room as if I never left it.

Month, September (No), a room. Who is living there? I reached the door of that room lost so far out of the way. Some years passed, the thought that the villa was gone. I knocked on the door. A man answered. He looked at me opening the door part way to question the traveler. Who are you? What do you want? I came back to find you, the woman said. Do you remember?

Mané led me into the room as dark as the shadows. It was a room from another time, the gray haired man touching my hair. I was overwhelmed by a sweet scent, as familiar as he was, the notes of tangerine, night jasmine and frangipane. Something else I detect. Tiare blossom, its sweetness clinging to coconut oil which blended rising with the heat from the earth, only to spill over, oiling our skin.

I stayed there with him caught in the moment, a virile magnetism brought true to life, by the voice whose rhythm was deep with the enigma of this soft earth and deep ocean. As if the room had been destined for sex and had been wrapped with a flash of red, and filled with flowers, freesias in a jar, on the window ledge, beneath it a bed covered with a dark red blanket. wall with white art paper rolled up on a desk.

He had only solitude as company. What does that mean for an artist? He could smash his head against the wall and scream until no one came, the walls closed in and the loneliest time of his life in this room.

I went back to the street to find you, I said.

What did you find? Mané asked.

I found none of that wind. And yet there was evidence it had pushed against the trees, with force, the pine needles on the pavement accumulated with a sharp sound. The house where we first made love, was about to be torn down, in the streets where we lived. Its paint blistered, the rain had damaged the fascia, but the house had stood waiting for this moment of reunion. The face of the mountain has not changed, the wall remains, the trees have grown. What do I notice? The house gone. Where the dreamer's dream, the bees left, death waits. I have left behind hearts and tiny arrows, I have left behind the contour of your warm body.

What else did you find?

181

An old manuscript stained with memory. At first, he did not notice the yellowing paper.

When things are unexpected, they appear to be in place and out of place at the same time. So the mind may not understand what the eyes see. The name of the Artist has been added into the manuscript but the woman's name is simply contained in the underpinnings of velum. The Artist is mentioned throughout the text. For it was only when the Artist is initiated by circumstances, when he reads the text, that he understands everything the woman feels about him.

Many things she has not disclosed before now, because she did not know them. Its primeval transmarine river, the schools of fishes all silvery aureoled slippery with stored up genetic information. I heard the sound of a child conceived with its soft sound, deep secrets of her growing. Everything we perfected and then repeated. The poet's heart. There was a tiny drop of blood, like miniature orbs of glistening berries. Gone the stain of love. The room where we conceived her no longer existed. I am guessing my way back to his bed, rather than saying good-bye.

Whether she left the manuscript on the table for him to find is an interesting question. As he read, moment by moment, the woman, strips down bare and reveals herself... she made life beautiful, because she could do it, because she wants to, maybe because she knows everything. Tell me how you remember it, Mané asked.

By sound mostly. The ancient foam as it pushed up on the shore. And the smell of newly washed sand. It was a sparsely populated area with the surf breaking on the reefs nearby. Restructuring the years, in its surf, the sound of waves that come and go. Sometimes I felt as if I had fallen into your arms and dreaming there, with the man who caught me, the smile of some erotic secret, flirting and the other with the hurt eyes of the man who had opened the door.

Sleepily, making love I could feel your hands touching manuscripts and papers, like poems within the sacrament of sex, typewritten, to the origins of pleasure. The rhythmic sound of noisy sex, oiled and slapping, once we were alone, before long, what was it? The warmth went to the bone. No one reminded us.

They're just vaporous words of the *Memoir for a Lover*, first written as a poem, tiny rectangles of typography, ink dabbed onto some piece of paper, words are making all these memories come back, words remember this rich and bare love. The blanket and pillows, ironed sheets, I imagine forever, sleeping with you, that soft cotton against bare skin.

Clarity to breasts, thighs, lips, together, a drawing, the Artist thought, sexy imagery remains for an afternoon, as taken as stolen when you looked through the window frame, with red freesias on the sill, summer light soaks orange citrus cast, deeply, whole afternoon, framing harlequin grill.

She being a beautiful woman. One sable brush stroke he would make, over her whole beautiful length, he could draw how he sees her, since his drawing embraces all forms of her: and he frames what he sees, a face exquisitely turned, the parting of lips on double red divide. He keeps framing the woman, in his head, in his mind, looking at light and shadows tracing back to some primitive cosmology of cave drawing, where each drawing has to do with natural form; if one describes deep chasms and earths own fire; what effect heat has on a body. He wanted to make love to her again, among heat, flute & birdsong.

Places remember us as we slowly forgot (one winter of anger beyond) when one long season defined remoteness (the blowing of the wind driven and pressed against us, the thickest and densest part of atmosphere lies at ground level) and confined life to a delicate boundary (because the thin line passes closest to you), I wept, they heard me, the only way a woman weeps, the way she turns towards you (rope me into your shadow please) and as I moved, you felt me press down, my hips there, it was a shaded scene, seasonal grasses on a slope, (cool green & bare woods) and so many shadows on one branch, I began to count the depth of shadow until our bodies filigree,(it is rarified, this change in atmosphere, the closer I get to you). You are still beautiful, Mané said. Drugged by this afternoon and all nights, I find her there. The kapok has held her shape as if she always existed, transformed into other women, she lives on. Perhaps forever. A man cannot wear her out. She will always exist. This physical pleasure. What is it? Is she the sum of silk underwear, a perfume, a taste, a touch as it dissolves like salt or sugar does. In a mouth.

Was she a woman scribed in kisses, cross-referenced to afternoon appointments of pleasure like delicate poems magnified by night's essence? In the celebration of wine, the bottle drowning in melted ice. Everything is just as I remembered it.

When he woke, his hands were warm under her body.

Have I changed much? I asked.

He turned his head to look at me. He looked as if he was trying to restore a faded fresco. She was holding a bottle of drinking water and wearing a blue cotton shirt. It was faded. Her hair cropped short. Her face pale. Paper shadows under her green eyes.
Not at all.
Nothing has changed to disorientate my memory or disfigure it, the Artist said. Everything enters my eyes. I know your body with my eyes closed. My thoughts seem to magnify how I see you, like water through a glass. The walls the color of cantaloupe melons where you have been. Thread count on indigo linen, a thousand stitches to every silk inch measured to the template of a tiny pinhead. So much time, but who is counting? Of course. Mané said softly. I have changed. We both have.

We reach out and just lie there in this joining, hips and lips. As a sense inside our bodies, holding another perfectly; moving closer to the inlet, closer still... loves warm pool, pulls us back from lonely. If love is a work of our own composition, it has always remained there, the genesis of us traced back through the rooms and the window frames, and the doorways, after the drawings, after the beaches, and small signs like the shoes left at the back door – and if you take steps away from this, the moments remain, after the perfume, after the candles and the linen sheets were tangled and twined with the meaning underlying all the sexual artifacts, they are beautiful by their intimate design. This is the grace of remembered things.

Your perfume still follows me, you are the only woman I feel whose blood runs through my own veins, as the body of love. I could be separated from you and yet still be with you. As close as this is. But not only in this room. When you are in love with one of its inhabitants, the room becomes a world. In this bed we hold together, and when we speak our words drifted on this beach of fallen water. This mended template of our sex, holding us in the physical world, the song of us, the falling of eyelids before sleep. Holding shadows in your fingers, inside the conception, behind the emotion, blind before our eyes returned as the constant river, holding us.

Looking back at him through a mask of water, real, existing. And the way you hair falls across my face like soft shadow. Inside my desire and the orgasm, between the sex and the way the binding tightens the drum of my skin. You are musk, the smell of a woman fills your bedroom. Slow suck of earth and the way you enter me, the seed in the core, the message in the code. The way we exist before we were lovers. Some voices made dents in heaven, in repetition of things more seductive than fallen angels.

For I have known this genesis, who has known to love you was a work of our own composition. Have known this ring and this love affair, we are part of each other, this will explain the first tributaries, like first love running its own course. To match my mouth to your mouth. Your tongue in my mouth, the boundaries diminishing. In this burning. The erotics of memory.

You would come with an offering of some kind, I said. Not perfume. Not flowers. Maybe white lace covered in scented rose petals and wrapped in pink tissue. As she pulls them up and two buds appear, the scent of roses in her lap, the outline of a soft entrance, he remembers the distance between. Each seam of her.

I have measured this love like a string of summer dreams, the dreams run through my mind, echoes us when we given this place to lie down in. When you dream, you kiss me when I am not there, make love without moving.

The bedroom becomes a pagoda of love, empty wine glasses, enigmas of intimacy, while his breathing fills the room. The sheets in the bedroom, crisp white linen, delicate flower patterns with thousands of fine threads, pulled together and cut not with scissors but seamstress teeth. If you look closely, you can see a tiny imprint of an incisor.

And yet it feels natural to be here, not improvised or contrived, unpremeditated, not contrived or planned. Falling into perfumed lakes and red rivers, drowning in the dreams of this place. It is not so important what happened but the passions and moments of beauty. Each is a moment of experience, an image. But I am not sure how you feel. If numbness and emptiness hold the same weight. How you felt about letting go, he whispered You had to think about so many things. But don't have to worry about loosing a chain of events. I know you. You work with emotions and impressions. If you hover between poetry and fiction this form of narrative might resolve it. You can narrate and poeticize, about the year we fell into love and beyond that.

She cannot leave memory behind, but carries it on her body, like a shroud it covers everything, like layers of linen, but roughly woven from the inside. I felt the quiet sigh, the deep labyrinth of sadness, angels... come back find us, if you can bear to look down on us. Come back.

Wait! What do you see? I see white for the first time, sharpened against the blue sky.

Early morning and late night - times closest to the anvil of dreams. But not those dreams All the long nights have fallen into places he now remembers. The Artist looked at the last page. The blank one. She has not written there. And so it makes sense to leave the last page blank. It makes the eyes skip the fine print.

I am about to ask you, to write a chapter in this book- to ask you to change what happens to you... you are able to do this, because images are changeable, you can add to them and subtract. It's only a dream: but I am about to ask you to bring the dreams back. And this is something you can do. Lovers swimming. The lover swims about a centimeter from her face, as close as possible without actually kissing; then their hands, the waves pushing and pulling back and forth, pushing them closer as into a tight space- until sea foam and their sweat formed a circle stretched around them. You could not tell one substance from the other. Until Mané moved through the water to kiss her. Then the taste of salt. He kissed her where the ocean fell away at the edge of the world. The world went red as the sea caught the sun flame. It burned like fire on water.

There is no one to hold us down. And you... you become the world, my remaining earth. We will not enter our own home or live in our native country, and when we die, our bones will be scattered in some other part of the world. But does it matter. We enter and leave together, between earth and a little rain. The first thought is of the wet flowering of the desert. of the warm pools of moisture that lie under your body, after we have made love .It is hot and wet., the smells here are so ancient, sweet and familiar. Full of seeds, basil, rice and rose petal tea.

Mané opens the French door to the balcony, then gardenia and frangipani collide in the room, white perfume falling over a pillow. The scent slipping slowly into his mind and in his thoughts, I will find original outline of you, he thought, it will be here, any time after dark, I will see in your eyes when you wake ,like a forgotten grain of sleep deep in the corners.

Late afternoon with her, in this oriental bed lacquered with rice fields & gold temples, she is beginning to wake, while the three women downstairs are peeling garlic & green shallot and stirring evening broth over coal fires. The warm scent floats upwards, painting the air with reds, greens and blues. Then red chili seed& fresh squeezed lime.

Mané, she said, how long have I been sleeping?

EPILOGUE

When the Poet's folio was published two years after her death, it was rumored to disclose her private life. A closer look confirmed that the secrets were still there in intricate boarders, each lion, angel, tree, a beautiful yet serious addition. The tiny etchings within the text have purpose. They are not just decoration. These intricate etchings enable the text to be understood beyond words, for gardens of flowers & wild animals& ascending angels', to be understood by the initiated.

As well as an intimate folio passed down to Dumas, Fifth Folio became a template to be carried forward by circumstances given to her to do so: She placed notations at the beginning of each section, the stains found and bindings are written, as pages pass through history, embellished, amended, torn, omitted, damaged and time changes what was. She sees these markers as clues, points of reference for direction in life. For her, a great personal war ended, her struggle with the contrast of intimacy, sexuality, power, injustice and loss in a personal code.

On the strength of the word before her, and all the Poet's who were exiled and died alone, she took the notes and named the Fifth Folio as her life work. It's like a statue, a Venus without arms, unearthed and having to be figured out, divined. The external, not intact, remains as fragment : intricate labyrinth of Fifth Folio became a reflection of her self. They are not every woman's secret as each woman's code may vary, but there are places in text all women will know. The weaving of time & incident, gaps & repetitions, as writing's exposé of intimate relationship, is merely a reflection of emotional content at the time of editing, as a the Fifth Folio was less than two hundred pages of the 10,000- page transcript of the original, held in safe deposit boxes in a London bank vault.

In June 2005, during the heat of humid summer in Hanoi, she suffered from pneumonia and spent two months in the French-Vietnamese Hospital. The malady continued and caused her to return to France a year later. Hoping to recover in the warmth of summer in the countryside, she was again hospitalized. During the second editorial process, the Poet knew she was dying. Against doctor's advice, she left France and returned to Hanoi. She arrived back at Villa Hanoi. September.

Looking at her laying beside him, he could draw her as he saw her now, observing the symmetry of her bare limbs, the tanned skin burnished and in parts, where skin forms into dimples at the lightest pressure or that the touch could first hold, and as he touched that exactness of shape, in the fall of it towards the thighs, where the waist ends and the rounding swell of the hips begins, then slide over a smooth surface and her thighs felt polished, copper in original colors, when he slid his hands between; and when he reached out and touched the beautiful growth of dark hair, in short soft curls, but it was no ordinary feeling, wheat fell into his palm and ripened and he separated the glistening seeds out with his finger. He looked around, there was no river, no field, no wind, only a woman's breathing.

For it is said, the personal life deeply lived, expands into truths beyond itself and with the inevitability of her death the poet may have provided her own answer to the question of a woman's existence.

190

SLEEPING WITH THE ARTIST
Nhà xuất bản Thế Giới
46 Trần Hưng Đạo - Hà Nội - Việt Nam

Chịu trách nhiệm xuất bản: Trần Đoàn Lâm
Biên tập: Đông Vĩnh
Trình bày: Ngô Thế Quân

In 500 bản (lần 1), khổ 14.5 x 20.5cm tại Xí nghiệp in Fahasa,
774 Trường Chinh, Phường 15, Q.Tân Bình, Tp.HCM, Việt Nam.
Giấy chấp nhận đăng ký kế hoạch xuất bản số 683-2007/CXB/
23-197/ThG, cấp ngày 10/09/2007. In xong và nộp lưu chiểu tháng 9/2007